HAWKWOOD

Also by Jonathan Guy

BADGER ISLAND
RAK: the story of an Urban Fox
PYNE

HAWKWOOD

Jonathan Guy

Julia MacRae Books

LONDON SYDNEY AUCKLAND JOHANNESBURG

*This book is for Kevin Pilsworth
who lives on the edge of Hopwas Wood*

First published 1996

1 3 5 7 9 10 8 6 4 2

Copyright © 1996 Jonathan Guy

Jonathan Guy has asserted his right
under the Copyright, Designs and Patents Act, 1988
to be identified as the author of this work

First published in Great Britain 1996
by Julia MacRae
an imprint of Random House
20 Vauxhall Bridge Road, London SW1V 2SA

Random House Australia (Pty) Ltd
20 Alfred Street, Milsons Point, Sydney, NSW 2061, Australia

Random House New Zealand Ltd
18 Poland Road, Glenfield, Auckland, New Zealand

Random House South Africa (Pty) Ltd
PO Box 337, Bergvlei 2012, South Africa

Random House UK Limited Reg. No 954009

A CIP catalogue record for this book is
available from the British Library

ISBN 1 85681 652 4

Photypeset by Intype, London
Printed and bound by
Mackays of Chatham PLC, Chatham, Kent

Contents

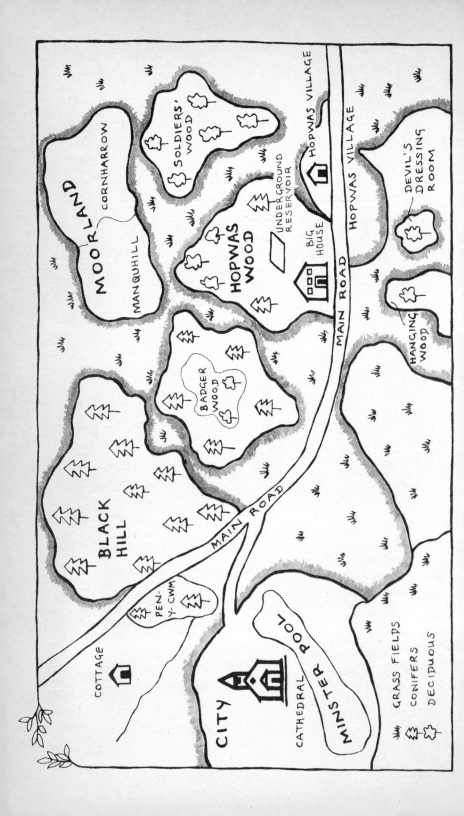

Part One

CONSERVATION

Chapter One

The woodpigeons roosting in the tall pines stirred with the coming of dawn, a fluttering of wings and shuffling on the boughs. Food was their only thought, they remembered the fields beyond the forest where they had fed throughout the previous day, spilled grain from the late harvest, some patches of corn that had been spoiled by the summer storms left standing. But it was too early to leave their nocturnal sanctuary yet.

Impatiently, the grey birds watched the sky, saw how it grew lighter and then became tinged with a pale rose colour that heralded the sunrise. Only when the early morning sunlight bathed the dark green foliage did the first woodpigeons leave their roost with a loud flapping of wings; they soared, gained height and then glided down the slopes of the steep valley.

The birds did not all depart together; timid by nature, it was the boldest which left first. The others watched the first pair go, then a single pigeon followed in their wake; two more, a bunch of half a dozen which had roosted on the same lofty branch flew together. Single birds began to leave at intervals. In spite of their empty crops and gnawing hunger, they seemed almost reluctant to begin a new day. Because every day had its dangers.

By the time the sun had topped the distant wooded horizon only one pigeon remained in that dark forest, a late-hatched fledgling which had not long learned to fly. His parents had no interest in him now, they no longer waited for him to accompany them out to the morning feed.

The young bird's powers of flight were strengthening with every passing day, he flapped his way clear of the trees. There was not another pigeon in sight, none for him to follow at a distance, but his sense of direction did not fail him. Somewhere down there the other pigeons would be busy gleaning.

A shadow fell across the now gliding pigeon but it only became aware of the danger when it was too late.

A huge fierce-looking bird hurtled downwards out of a sky that a few seconds before had been devoid of life. It dived with all the speed and accuracy of a bolt fired from a crossbow. Sunlight glinted upon Garn's barred breast, blunt wings arrowing his deadly flight. The pigeon panicked but had no time to take evasive action; the goshawk struck in mid-flight, the pigeon's loose plumage billowing in the manner of a burst pillow, feathers floating in the air as vicious talons closed its outstretched wings and held it captive.

Without so much as a pause or a change of direction, Garn bore his early morning catch down into a disused slate quarry. This marauder of the skies fed ravenously before flying off back to the forest which had been his home for as long as he could remember.

Garn and his mate, Ka, roosted together in a tall pine tree on the edge of a dark Russian forest. Night or day, they were seldom apart from each other, for goshawks mate for life, hunt together except during the breeding season – when Garn was the provider whilst Ka sat on her eggs and reared her chicks. Then, when the young departed the nest to fend for themselves, the parent birds resumed their inseparable companionship. They knew no other way of life.

The breeding season was now long gone and the autumn nights were cold. The goshawks' thoughts turned to Winter and survival.

Here, Winter began early and lasted right through to April; snow drifted and froze with the hardness of icebergs, grew in size with each succeeding blizzard. When the thaw finally came it took weeks for the snow to melt. There were no sudden thaws, it was a land of dark forests and winter wastelands.

Food was scarce during these long bitter months and often Garn and Ka were forced to feed along with the buzzards on the remains of a deer pulled down by a pack of ravenous wolves; or a rabbit on the verge of starvation that had dug its way out of its burrow to gnaw the bark on a frozen tree. The woodpigeons migrated with the coming of Autumn, deserted these forests for warmer climates. The starlings followed them, noisy quarrelsome birds which fouled the woodlands and disturbed the peace of night with their incessant twittering. Their flesh was rancid, the hawks did not bother them. They might have done so, though, had the starlings remained here in the winter for then any freshly killed meat was welcome.

The chill wind rustled the dying foliage, strengthened and tore the leaves from the boughs, blew them into piles in sheltered places. Clouds scudded across a starlit sky; there were a few spots of rain in the wind.

But the pine trees on the edge of the forest gave the roosting goshawks protection from the elements, they did not mind stormy nights; there would be plenty of those in the ensuing months.

Garn heard a movement down below. It was probably a wild boar grubbing for roots, digging up the ground with its sharp tusks. Or perhaps a wolf scavenging. Or even a bear. There were always night noises in the forest.

Further along the branch Ka shifted uneasily, she was always nervous at night. She shuffled nearer her mate. Not

5

that she had any idea what that danger might be, hers was an instinctive fear of the darkness and the unknown terrors which might lurk in it.

A twig cracked beneath the birds. Ka started, hissed. Garn, fully alert now, stared at the silhouettes of branches swaying and creaking in the wind. Whatever it was down there, it could not possibly harm them for only grey squirrels scaled these tall trees. And squirrels were a delicacy, they tasted much the same as rabbit, if you were fortunate enough to catch one. But squirrels did not venture from their dreys or holes in hollow tree trunks after dark.

What was it then that moved below?

The pine tree shook slightly, it was probably the wind. Garn prepared to go back to sleep. But another crack, much louder this time, had Ka edging right up against him. She was trembling.

Something was climbing up the pine tree.

Ka was terrified, only the darkness prevented her from flying off in panic. Night was the captor of all birds of prey – with the exception of owls who hunted then. Garn was erect, listening, his sharp talons gripped the branch, gouged it.

There was a scraping, slipping noise as if the intruder had missed a foothold; a branch groaned beneath the climber as it was grabbed to prevent a fall. Certainly it was no small creature; bears were known to clamber up into low branches but they were cumbersome animals who had no head for heights.

Now, whatever it was, was only two or three boughs away from the terrified birds. Again, Ka hissed a warning, during the night hours she could not make her high-pitched cry. Be still and await your fate, you have no choice! Without light it was impossible for them to fly to safety; darkness rendered them helpless, at the complete mercy of any enemy which was able to reach their roost; they could not even protect themselves with raking talons or stabbing beaks.

The intruder was large and heavy from the way the branches creaked beneath its weight, as big as a boar yet boars were unable to climb. The bough upon which the goshawks roosted shook. They gripped it tightly for fear of being dislodged, afraid of falling and fluttering to the forest floor way below where they would be at the mercy of whatever beast chanced upon them.

Their perch bowed, the intruder had secured a grip on it. Ka was pressed tightly against Garn. They heard laboured breathing, a grunting that was neither bear nor boar; smelt a scent which was unfamiliar to them but was undoubtedly the sour stench of danger.

Suddenly, a dazzling light blinded both birds. Ka was gripped, held tightly; it was impossible even to flutter her wings at the peak of her terror. Garn felt his mate being lifted from him; he remained motionless, powerless to help her.

Ka was gone and now it was his turn. He was seized, plucked from his perch, felt as though he was being crushed as his wings were held tightly. One moment there was blinding white light, the next complete darkness. Then the grip on him was relinquished, he was aware of a suffocating atmosphere and he was lying on top of his shaking mate in a tiny enclosed place. Their prison was of some kind of loose material that shut out even the starlight and smelled of strange and frightening odours. The goshawks made no attempt to struggle, they just lay there bewildered and frightened.

A sound came from their captor as the tricky descent began; it was not the grunting of a wild animal and yet it was vaguely familiar, like the noises that the peasants made when they came to the forest to gather fallen branches.

Man!

Garn and Ka had come to accept humans at a distance; they had never presented a threat but the birds were wary of them. Garn realized now, without any doubt, that it was humans who had come to the forest under cover of darkness, climbed the tall pine and taken the goshawks from their roost.

Why? He had no idea but capture was a terrifying prospect to a creature who had never known anything other than freedom. Enclosed in a heavy sack, the hawks were aware that they were being taken somewhere far from the forest which had been their only home.

Vehicles were beyond their understanding, they did not associate the engine noise, the stench of exhaust fumes with the occasional tractor that came to drag fallen trees from the forest. They huddled together throughout the long journey, struggled to breathe in their stifling prison.

They gave up all hope.

It was daylight before the vehicle finally came to a halt, the engine stuttering and dying. As Garn was lifted out of the sack, he clawed in a token protest at the hands which held him but his talons scraped harmlessly on thick leather gauntlets. Ka offered no resistance.

There were two men who conversed in sounds that were meaningless to the captured hawks. Even so, their tone and actions were of satisfaction, they were clearly well pleased with their night's work.

Garn blinked and stared at the rows of mesh cages that lined the gloomy interior of the wooden building. The majority of these were occupied, birds that sat on perches regarded the newcomers with mild curiosity. Every one of them was a hawk of some kind. Garn recognized them as fellow hunters in his native homeland; a majestic buzzard that had once soared on ragged, moth-like wings, relying on guile rather than speed to catch its prey; a sparrowhawk which bore a remarkable similarity to the goshawks except that it was much smaller; a kite with a long forked tail; an eagle that perched sorrowfully, doubtless pining for the mountains where it had once ruled supreme over lesser birds of prey and had been the nemesis of small mammals.

Now all of these hunters of the wild were reduced to a state of dejection, sat motionless and hunched with ruffled feathers, ignominious in captivity, deprived of their regal way of life and relegated to eating the kill of others, fed to them by Man.

Garn and Ka were put in an empty cage. At least they were imprisoned together, that was a small consolation.

There were journeys by road and rail. And air. The latter was worst of all, a cramped hold where air was scarce and the darkness was darker than they had ever known before.

They sensed that they were airborne, a familiar feeling of altitude amidst the droning of the powerful engines and the vibration and rattlings of the bodywork. Strongest of all was their feeling of helplessness. Oh, how they longed to fly with their own wings, to dive and swoop, to hunt and kill. The loss of their freedom was worse than death.

Their next imprisonment was worse than any they had known since their capture. The rows of cages held a variety of birds, many of them exotic species with brightly coloured plumages who made incessant loud calls that bore a remarkable similarity to the voices of their human captors. There were small birds, too, which stared in amazement at the goshawks and mocked them in a manner which they would not have dared to do in the open woods and fields.

There were adjacent sheds where dogs yapped and whined by day and night, and an enclosure where giant cats paced restlessly throughout the daylight hours, giving ferocious roars of rage and frustration.

It seemed to Garn and Ka that every creature here was unhappy. Every day was the same as the one that had gone before and the nights were long and dark and noisy. Until one day Garn and Ka were taken from their cage, lifted with gloved hands and transferred to a box that was just big enough for both of them. Shafts of daylight slanted in through small holes in the lid; it was not possible to see outside.

The journey by road was long and tedious, the atmosphere was heavy with those strange unpleasant smells which the birds had experienced before. Stopping and starting, seemingly going nowhere in particular. They had learned by now that there would be another cage awaiting them wherever they arrived.

The journeys, the different prisons, were a nightmarish blur in the goshawks' confused memories; an eternity. Perhaps life had always been like this and the fir forest was but a longing for a place that did not exist.

Sometimes, on dark nights, when their surroundings were not starkly visible, Garn and Ka smelled that sweet aroma of resin, heard the mewing of a buzzard over the pines, or breathed in the foulings of the starlings on the undergrowth. This unclean building had a similar odour. It reminded Garn and Ka of reality.

They were very homesick.

This time it was a much larger aviary where there was enough space to flap from one perch to another, to stretch wings that had grown weak after a lengthy period of inactivity. There were no other birds or animals within sight or sound.

The goshawks did not know how long they would be kept here, the prospect never occurred to them. They had learned to take each day and night as it came. Certainly, they would never see their homeland again.

The humans here were different, much kinder; they appeared to be interested in the hawks' welfare rather than just feeding and watering them twice a day. Particularly the tall man whose loose-fitting clothes had a faint smell of pine trees. He came into the building regularly, sometimes stayed for some considerable time just watching them. He talked to them, too, and although they had no idea what he was saying, his tone was almost reassuring. Not that the goshawks trusted any human after their capture and imprisonment.

One morning the tall man brought a companion with him.

The other was shorter, wore clothes that, even to the birds who regarded him warily, did not relate to the wild. His bearing was one of authority, the tall one nodded frequently, spoke little.

"A fine pair," the newcomer peered through the mesh, a pipe clenched between his teeth giving off pungent fumes. "I'd say these are superior to that pair last year."

The tall man's head bobbed, his hands were folded behind his back. "I agree with you, sir. Superb breeding stock." The man knew that only the previous year a pair of goshawks had had their eggs stolen by poachers and had then been shot and stuffed as trophies.

"Release them on the same site as last year, Swift, the one on Black Hill. There's a chance they'll use the nest which the previous pair built. But you'll have to guard them, day and night. Take it in turns with Jackson. That gamekeeper, Reuben, will help, too, I'm sure. We can't afford to lose another pair and most of the rare nesting sites these days are known to egg thieves."

"We'll watch them . . . like hawks!" The forest ranger smiled at his own joke but his boss's expression remained stoic. "There's just one thing that worries me, sir."

"What's that?" The chief forester's head jerked round.

"Well," Swift shifted his stance uneasily, "according to the latest figures released, there's over five hundred breeding pairs of goshawks in Britain now. That figure could double in a year or two. Goshawks are rapacious hunters, it might be that . . . well, our songbird population could diminish as a result of a national concentration of hawks . . . even to the point of extinction." His lower lip trembled slightly, it was a brave man who questioned government forestry policies, especially with Timpson, the chief forester.

"Nonsense," the short man turned away from the cage, wagged a finger at his subordinate in undisguised admonishment. "Hawks are an integral part of the forestry's conservation policy, a public relations exercise, you should know

11

that, Swift. Just suppose that we concentrated our efforts on re-introducing small diminishing species into our forests, nightjars, skylarks, buntings etc., The public wouldn't even notice them on their weekend rambles! But they'll see hawks, all right, stand and marvel at them, some people even write in and congratulate us on our conservation successes! We must be *seen* to be conserving, Swift, that is the criteria, never mind the small birds. Do you understand now?"

"Yes, sir," Swift looked down at his feet, his reply was unconvincing.

"Good, that's settled, then. It is important that we are seen as a caring, conservation-minded organisation. The goshawks' nesting site must be protected to the exclusion of all else. If the birds use the old nest then an area of fifty acres surrounding the site must be designated an exclusion zone. I will advise the shooting tenant that he cannot shoot within its boundaries. He will doubtless complain, as he did last year, that he has paid rent for the acreage but conservation has priority over sporting activities. Now, I'll leave it to you to release these birds into the wild and monitor their progress. They will have a few weeks to find and renovate the old nest, or to build a new one if they prefer, before it is time to breed."

Garn and Ka watched the two men leave the outbuilding. The birds sensed that the discussion between the humans had something to do with their future. The future was always frightening.

It made them uneasy. They were not surprised, therefore, when the tall man returned some time later wearing heavy duty leather gauntlets. Yet there was a gentleness about the way he took the birds from the aviary and put them into a wicker carrying basket.

Once again they embarked upon their travels but this time, strangely, they had the feeling that they were about to arrive at their final destination.

Chapter Two

For a short time the goshawks believed that they had been returned to their native pine forest. Their initial reaction was one of disbelief when the tall forestry ranger and his young companion opened the carrying basket and retreated to the edge of the clearing.

The birds were wary, suspicious. They peered out, watched the two humans, then took in their surroundings. The odour of resin in the air was almost overpowering, just like it used to be. Some distance away they heard a steady whining; they remembered the sound, sometimes men came to the forest to cut down trees.

There was a flap of wings from one of the nearby trees; Garn glimpsed a woodpigeon clattering to safety. His instinct was to dart in pursuit, strike down his prey in full flight. But not this time, he was not ready for hunting yet.

The situation was disturbing, the way the two men watched fixedly as though they were waiting for something to happen. Somewhere a buzzard called, that familiar mewing. In the far distance crows cawed.

Nothing had changed, it was just like it always was.

Garn hopped up on to the side of the basket. Ka joined

him and their combined weight tilted the container so that it nearly toppled over. They sat there watching. Waiting.

Garn stretched his wings, realized how weak they had become during his lengthy captivity. He might just make it to the nearest tree. He hesitated, doubted his ability even to fly that far.

It was foolish to remain here, their captors might change their minds, shut them up again. Freedom was on offer, the hawks might never have the chance again.

Ka followed in the wake of her mate, propelled herself into the air, glided rather than flew and had to force her wings to lift her up on to a low bough alongside Garn. Together they perched, regarded the humans below. At least they were out of reach of their captors, they would not be caught easily.

The chief ranger nodded to his companion; then they picked up the empty basket and, without so much as a glance backwards, walked quickly away.

The goshawks realised then that they had been set free, there was no way that they would ever allow themselves to be captured again. When night approached they would find a roosting place that was inaccessible to Man. In their own way they were euphoric; had their wings been strong enough they would have flown and called loudly, let the whole forest know that they were back. But they knew that they were not strong enough yet.

Certainly this was the same forest in which they had been raised and had lived all their lives. The pines reached up to the sky, smelled the same; there were pigeons; a lone buzzard soared and wheeled with effortless ease high above. Everything was just as it had always been except... *something* was different. Garn and Ka were at a loss to know what it was, just an uneasy feeling, nothing more.

The chainsaws were suddenly silent; seconds later they heard a tree come crashing down. The chainsaws started up again.

When they were completely recovered from their enforced idleness and their wings had regained their full powers of flight, the goshawks would move on, explore, find a place as far from Man as possible. Until then they would be very vigilant.

It was definitely Spring; they recognised a warm dampness in the atmosphere, the wind no longer blew with the viciousness of the winter months. In fact, it was much warmer than usual for so early in the year. That was something else that puzzled them. Often there was still snow lying in places when the trees and undergrowth began to sprout again.

The goshawks practised short flights but their wings tired easily and they had to rest for long periods; once Ka had to plane down to the ground because she did not have the strength to reach the tree in which Garn had settled. He was tired, too.

On that first night they found a stunted fir growing out of the face of a disused slate quarry and they roosted there for the night; there was no way that any human could have climbed up to them. And if one tried then they would hear him scrabbling on the loose slate.

They dozed, never really slept, their instinctive wariness would warn them if danger approached. Below them nocturnal animals foraged, they recognised the rancid odour of a fox. Another creature grunted and snuffled, it was too light-footed for a bear and it was too early in the season for cubs. Its scent was similar to that of a bear, though. Owls hooted and screeched all around.

Day broke slowly, a grey light permeating the blackness of night. A chorus of waking woodpigeons reminded the goshawks just how hungry they were.

Pigeons began to flight overhead, heading for some distant field that offered breakfast, unsuspecting birds passing close to where the goshawks perched. Garn watched, tensed.

Garn launched himself from the branch, a flap of those stubby wings putting him on course for a pigeon that had just passed. He never anticipated any problems, he would catch it up, arrow in on his target, strike it down amidst a cloud of feathers.

He discovered to his dismay that he was not overhauling his intended prey; it kept ahead of him, it wasn't even aware that it was being pursued! Garn needed a sudden surge of power if he and Ka were to eat freshly-killed meat that morning, a wing thrust to give him additional speed.

But his wing muscles refused to respond. His wings opened but they were already tired, they slowed rather than speeded his sleek body. His quarry was pulling further away from him, he felt himself losing height; it was a strange and frightening sensation.

The woodpigeon disappeared from view over some tall trees. Garn knew that he could not make it over those fir tops, he glided towards the lower branches and settled. Ka was perched in a tree some distance behind him, her wings were even weaker than his own. Bewildered, they rested apart. The pigeon's escape had made them even hungrier than before.

Later that day Garn swooped on a rabbit that passed unsuspectingly beneath the tree. The goshawks fed ravenously together; the freshly-killed meat seemed to revive them.

It was towards evening that Garn and Ka became aware that this forest was not the same one that they had known throughout their lives. A short flight took them over the brow of a hill from where they had a full view of the countryside spread out below them.

Everywhere was so unfamiliar, everything about it was alien to the bemused hawks. There was no distant coastline, instead the land sloped gently down to a main road below. The traffic was constant, they had never seen so many vehicles in the whole of their lives before. There were scattered human dwellings, a patchwork of fields and smaller woods, a cluster of houses and a church spire that poked up above some sycamores.

Where *was* this strange place? They had no idea, only that it was far from the wooded mountainsides which they had hunted before their capture. This was Man's domain, he had even conquered the woods with his chainsawing. There was just one consolation.

They had regained their freedom.

Ka found the old nest at the very top of a larch tree on the south slope of Black Hill. Her maternal instinct guided her to it, a shallow platform of interwoven twigs that had a flimsy appearance yet it had defied the winter gales. It was the kind of place any hawk would seek out, high above the ground yet sheltered from the elements by a mass of closely growing branches that were just coming into bud. It was also an excellent vantage point, it offered a view of the forest below and as far as the distant village.

Within the hour Ka had begun to renovate that nest, bringing up twigs from the forest floor, weaving them into the structure as only a female hawk knew how. She knew without any doubt that it was one of her own kind who had used it last, a few bedraggled goshawk feathers adhered to the sides. If the previous occupant tried to return, Garn would drive it off. Likewise, he would put any other species of hawk to flight which dared to come near.

Garn's wings were regaining their former strength with each passing day, his hunting prowess had not been dulled by his period of captivity. He caught rabbits and voles and became the nemesis of pigeons and other smaller birds. Wherever this place was, it was to his liking. Prey was in abundance, far more than there had ever been in that other forest.

Ka completed her rebuilding work and began to lay. Within a week she had settled down to sit three eggs. Now Garn's task had doubled, it was necessary for him to catch enough food for both of them. Before long he would have a hungry brood to feed as well.

In the course of his hunting he explored even further; the Black Hill was the largest of the upland conifer woods. Up above, stretching beyond the horizon, was a tract of moorland. Garn hunted this high ground systematically, quartering the heather, and invariably flushed some red grouse. These were a worthy quarry; they gave him a good chase sometimes escaping by dropping down into the thick heather, squatting out of sight. Goshawks only killed in the open, they never pursued their prey into dense cover.

Below Black Hill was another large conifer plantation in the midst of which stood an area of mature oak and beech, a kind of island in an ocean of dark green firs. It fascinated the goshawk on occasions when he flitted through its silent mysterious interior. Once he caught a rabbit there; another time he glimpsed a large animal with a striped head. He had never seen such a creature before and he settled on a bough to watch it more closely. It scuttled along a well-worn track and then disappeared down a big hole in the ground. The creature reminded him of the bears in his homeland except that it was much smaller.

Garn observed the forestry workers, too. He perched in a tree on the slope above where they were felling trees. They had cut down a lot of trees, laid a whole area bare, just the stumps sticking up out of the brashings; the trunks were stacked in piles along a muddy track. Every day big lorries with winches came to take the timber away. The goshawk was concerned in case one day the chainsaws felled the larch where Ka was sitting her eggs. Most days he returned to the felling area to watch this desecration of the forest. Truly, Man had claimed it for his domain.

One morning whilst Garn was watching from his vantage point a Land Rover drove up to the felling area. A man climbed out and walked towards the foresters with an air of authority. He was the smaller of the two men who had come to look at the goshawks in captivity that day, the one whom the taller of the two appeared to be in awe of. As did these workmen who switched off their chainsaws and gathered around the newcomer.

This man did most of the talking, the others just listened, nodded their heads. He pointed several times towards the huge larch tree which stood starkly on the south-facing hillside. Everybody looked where he directed and Garn became concerned. Perhaps they knew that Ka nested there and they were going to cut the tree down. Or maybe return under cover of darkness and capture her on the nest. And he himself, too, for he always roosted close by. It was a worrying thought.

Then the man returned to his Land Rover and drove away down the muddy track. The men clustered together, talked amongst themselves. They were clearly disturbed and angry.

The men did not go back to their tree felling. Instead, they began gathering up their tools, stacked them in the back of the truck. They even dismantled the green canvas shelter in which they ate their sandwiches at mid-day. There was a dejection about their actions, an unwillingness which they had not shown in the presence of their boss.

Then they clambered aboard the truck and drove away. Garn returned to that place every day after that but the forestry workers had not come back. Perhaps they had tired of cutting down trees and had gone away to do something else. The goshawk did not understand but he was relieved that they had left.

However, the Black Hill forest was not without a human presence. Garn was aware that a man came on foot most days, followed the track up through the dense conifers that brought him up above the larch trees. Often he remained there for several hours, crouched in the undergrowth, looking from time to time through a pair of binoculars. He was watching Ka's nest with interest, rarely did he look elsewhere. It was the tall ranger.

Every day somebody came to that same place to watch the

nest, it was seldom free of a hidden observer. There was another human who came more furtively but this one avoided the paths and crept through the fir thickets. His vantage point was well away from that used by the rangers. Once Garn glimpsed his features but he did not recall having seen them before. This stranger worried him most, the man was so secretive.

There was far too much human interest in the goshawks for Garn's liking. Back home there had never been any interference before that night when they were captured.

Each day he became more uneasy. Had Ka not been sitting on her eggs, he would have persuaded her to fly to some place of greater safety, possibly beyond the high moorland. But Ka would not desert her nest and neither would Garn leave his mate. Nature decreed that the reproduction of a species was a priority and the goshawks obeyed their instincts. They had no choice, but they sensed that their freedom was restricted.

Ka knew that the eggs were close to hatching. Now she huddled more closely over them, scarcely acknowledging her mate when he flew up to her with food. And if she was aware that Man was watching her, she showed no sign.

Garn now hunted an area within close proximity of the nest. His instincts told him not to leave Ka unprotected. He sensed danger.

Chapter Three

*I*t was a wet night. Thick cloud formations had moved in on the prevailing wind throughout the afternoon and by evening a torrential downpour had begun. The forest foliage dripped steadily, turning the soft ground into a quagmire.

Ka sat impassively on her eggs, the weather was of no consequence to her, perhaps she did not even notice the rain. Garn roosted close by, hunched against the tree trunk. Like all land birds he hated wet weather but he accepted it. Far rather this than the dry, stuffy confinement of a cage.

A badger hurried below, eager to find food and return to the comfort of the sett; a dog fox caught a rabbit, Garn heard the pitiful squealings of the unfortunate victim.

And there were other noises, disturbing ones.

The goshawk was instantly alert. A heavy tread squelched in the mud, it was definitely neither badger nor fox. Something scraped against the tree trunk. The bough which supported the nest quivered slightly.

Garn tensed, remembered only too well how it had been that time before in the dark forest far from here. A branch snapped.

Then came a slithering sound, a grunt that was definitely human. Garn shuffled closer to the nest; Ka was a motionless, barely discernible silhouette against the stormy sky. She gave no sign that she had heard, her duty was to cover her eggs until they hatched. Nothing, not even death, would deter her.

A human was climbing the larch; he stood on a stout slippery bough, reached up to test another which would bear his weight. Garn smelled the sour stench of sweat, of fear. The man was afraid but that did not lessen the danger.

It was just as it had been the last time and now, as then, the birds were powerless to escape. Even had the moon been full with enough light for the goshawks to flap across to another tree, Ka would not have left her nest. And neither would Garn have sought his own safety. They would remain here and await their fate.

The intruder had almost reached them, he was only a couple of branches away and groping for another handhold. He was breathing heavily, muttering to himself.

Garn felt a hand brush against his legs. By day he would have raked viciously with his talons, stabbed with his beak. By night he did nothing.

Any moment that hand would close over him, pinion his wings and lift him from his perch, drop him into a suffocating sack. Instead, the hand passed on, gloved fingers feeling their way along the branch, until they found the nest.

Ka hunched, stiffened. She hissed her fear and anger but she made no attempt to peck at the probing fingers that pushed their way beneath her and explored the nest.

She felt one of the eggs move, she pressed down hard with her body but it made no difference. The hand was withdrawn; a few seconds later it returned. A second egg was removed. Just one remained and then those thieving gloved fingers were fumbling for it beneath her. They found it, took it.

The goshawks listened to the man descending the tree, splashing down into the mud. And then he was gone.

Panic erupted at first light in the goshawks' nest. Ka stretched her wings, gave a piercing cry.

Hi-aa-hi-aa.

She took off crazily, followed by Garn. His *ca-ca-ca* became a *gek-gek-gek* in his anger. They hurtled like arrows, weaving between the dripping trees, quartered, searching with eyes that missed nothing. A blackbird fled, screaming its terror, but for once these fierce hunters ignored it. A rabbit crouched, terror-stricken, as they flew past but this morning it was safe. The goshawks' thoughts were only for the stolen eggs and Nature's plan for the continuation of a species that had been re-introduced to Black Hill.

Garn and Ka flew relentlessly throughout that damp morning, the low cloud which had lingered on the hills in the wake of the rain hampered their futile search.

Yet again Man had betrayed them. The tree-cutters' encampment remained deserted.

On and on, Garn and Ka searched every ride, every thicket. From the upper reaches of Black Hill they scoured the moorland; then south to Hopwas Wood and the adjoining Soldiers' Wood. They rested for a time in Badger Wood before crossing the main road to the two spinneys, the Devil's Dressing Room and the Hanging Wood.

It was mid-afternoon when they returned to Black Hill only to discover that Man had once more invaded their adopted domain. In the clearing where the foresters used to park their machinery, two vehicles stood; a Land Rover with a blue beacon on its roof although the light was not flashing. Beside it was a green van with tree logos on its doors. The occupants of these vehicles had gone on foot to the tall larch where one of them was just climbing down from the nest. It was the tall forestry ranger.

Two men awaited his descent. One was the young ranger, the other was a uniformed police officer. To the goshawks they were all enemies to be feared.

Garn and Ka alighted in a pine tree some distance away,

remained motionless, watching. These men were clearly angry and disturbed, too. There was much talking and shaking of heads before, finally, they began walking slowly back to the parked vehicles.

Later that day Ka flew back up to the nest and settled herself down as though nothing had changed, as if there had been no theft and the eggs were still there waiting to be incubated.

Garn did not disturb her, at least she was more settled than she had been earlier in the day. His only fear was that the thief, having stolen the eggs, might return for the parent birds.

They really should find another home but it was only too evident that Ka had no intention of leaving the nest in the larch tree.

Just as dusk was deepening the green van with the tree pictures on its doors drove slowly up the forest track. Garn watched with dismay, again he feared for their safety. The eggs were gone, there was no reason for Ka to stay on the nest. But she squatted there stoically, perhaps she even refused to accept that her unhatched young had been snatched from her.

It was still light enough to glide silently away, perhaps roost in that tree on the quarry face. He stretched his wings, looked at her. She was staring fixedly ahead of her; if she had seen, then his suggestion had been ignored.

Garn resigned himself to another night on this vulnerable roost. If the thief returned and took Ka, then Garn would go with her. He would not want to be left alone.

The van driver took care to park his vehicle off the muddy track behind a clump of dense undergrowth. The wheels spun, he revved the engine, somehow managed to slew the van up a slight incline.

Satisfied that it could not be seen from the muddy track, he reached out a thermos and a pack of sandwiches, locked the doors and trudged towards that same observation point which he had used throughout the failed nesting vigil.

It was going to be a long and uncomfortable night for Jackson, the assistant forestry ranger. The chief had ordered a round-the-clock watch on the goshawks; he was furious that the eggs had been taken. If the birds themselves were to be stolen or harmed then jobs would be in jeopardy and the junior ranger's was the most likely to go. Only a scapegoat would satisfy the forestry hierarchy if anything else went wrong. Their conservation project was fast falling apart.

Even Reuben, the gamekeeper for the syndicate which rented the shooting rights over the surrounding area, had been asked to take part in protecting these rare birds and none knew the forest better than he.

Jackson had reservations about Reuben's involvement where rare birds were concerned; he was a ruthless man whose only concern was his pheasants. If anything harmed them, then they were shot or trapped, and goshawks were notorious predators. That was a worrying factor but it was none of Jackson's business; he was paid to obey orders, not to question them.

The ranger checked his infra-red night glasses and settled himself down as comfortably as was possible. The rain had passed on but it was a damp and misty night, there would probably be a thick hill fog by morning which would make his task all the more difficult.

Chapter Four

*T*he two youths glanced furtively around. They had parked their motor cycles in a lay-by on the main road, cut across the fields, skirted Badger Wood and in due course they had arrived on the south slope of Black Hill.

They were dressed in waterproof clothing and wore green rubber boots. There was a similarity about their features; they were undoubtedly brothers, they might even have been twins.

They stopped and looked about them. The long pine needle-carpeted track was deserted as far as they could see and the only sound was that of rain dripping off the trees. A heavy shower had drenched the undergrowth and passed on. With trembling fingers they unslung the gunslips from their shoulders, fumbled with the fasteners. Just as these two looked alike, so were their weapons identical, heavy high-powered air-rifles fitted with telescopic sights.

"I don't like it," the one whispered hoarsely. "They say the police were up 'ere the other day."

"Who says?"

"Our dad 'eard it in the Red Lion."

"Well, you can never believe what our dad says, nor what them lot in the Lion says, neither. 'Cept there's a pair o' eagles moved in up 'ere and I know that's right 'cause I caught a glimpse of them flyin' over the wood from the road."

"We'll get into trouble for shootin' 'em, Ian."

"Not if nobody knows, we won't."

"You can't eat *eagles*!"

"Stupid! We ain't goin' to eat 'em. We're goin' to stuff 'em and sell 'em. I saw on the telly a while back that a stuffed eagle fetched a grand and it was eighty years old. Imagine what a *fresh* stuffed one would fetch! All the same, we 'ave to be careful. Now, I reckon they're usin' that big larch tree up there, that's about where I saw 'em. We'll 'ave to go quietly."

They began to creep slowly along the ride. The saturated pine needles squelched under their feet. They passed beneath a tall Scots pine. Had they glanced up they might have seen the objects of their interest perched at the top, regarding them suspiciously. But both Ian and his brother, Ben, were intent on watching the larch tree.

"If we hide under that larch and wait, the eagles are sure to come back eventually. They're probably off hunting right now. Let 'em settle. You take one, I'll take the other."

"S'pose we don' kill 'em?" Ben was nervous, he wished that he hadn't come.

"That's even better, we'll sell 'em live, get more for 'em like that. We'll throw our jackets over 'em and . . ."

"Ian . . ." Ben stopped suddenly.

"What now? We gotta keep quiet, no talkin'."

"Ian . . . *there's somebody comin'*!"

Ian stopped, stared, his heartbeat stepped up a gear. Ben was right, there was somebody walking down the track towards them.

"Who is it, Ian?"

"How would I know? But we'll soon find out," Ian mounted his air-rifle to his shoulder, looked down the telescopic sight. The magnification brought the approaching man's features right up close, they were only too recognisable at a hundred metres. Ian pursed his lips, his pulses going like triphammers.

"Who is it, Ian? Is it a copper?"

"No," Ian's voice shook as he answered. Far rather had it been a policeman than the man who strode belligerently towards them. "It's . . . it's *Reuben*!"

Ben paled. He thought about making a run for it but changed his mind; it was too late, the custodian of the game preserves over Black Hill and Hopwas Wood was bearing down on them. Reuben carried his shotgun and, if his reputation was anything to go by, he would not hesitate to pepper their legs if they tried to escape.

"Oi, you! What's the idea of pointing that gun at me!" Reuben wore camouflage clothing, had he stood amongst the trees he would have been virtually invisible. His coarse features were flushed with anger, his cruel lips curled in a sneer.

"I was . . . just usin' the 'scope as a telescope." Ian swallowed, all his former bravado was gone, he was very frightened.

"Oh, yeah! You were goin' to take a pot shot at me . . . until you noticed my gun and thought you might get sommat more'n you bargained for back. Now, *I* know what you're after, and I also know what you've been and done, so you'd better come clean."

"We wasn't goin' to *shoot* the eagles," Ben whined. "We was just goin' to look at them. Bird watchin', that's what we was doin'."

"Watching 'em through your 'scopes and then pull the trigger, eh?" The gamekeeper laughed harshly. "Eagles, you think?"

"They said in the pub that there was eagles on Black Hill."

Reuben looked heavenwards. "I'm not here to give you lessons in ornithology. Now, hand me those guns."

The air-rifles were passed over meekly. Both youths stood subdued.

"Right," Reuben clasped the weapons in one hand, kept his shotgun in the crook of his arm. "You'd better tell me what you've done with them eggs?" His eyes narrowed, his expression was menacing.

"*Eggs!*" Ian and Ben looked aghast. "What eggs? We ain't . . ."

"I know that you stole them. You climbed that tree the other night, took the eggs from under the sitting bird, then you thought you'd come back and get the hawks. That was your big mistake."

"No, honest . . ."

"*Don't lie!*" Reuben shouted. Then, somehow, he got himself back under control. "Well, I hardly expected you to admit to it. But, you will . . . I'm taking you to the forestry headquarters where, doubtless, Mr Timpson will call the police. We'll see how you get on then, eh! There's a fine of two thousand pounds for stealing goshawk eggs and you might even go to prison as well . . ."

The gamekeeper signalled to the youths to walk in front of him back the way they had come. Their shoulders were hunched, their heads were bowed. A cunning smile flitted across his features. Maybe this pair would confess under pressure, they were the sort. At any rate, as far as the foresters and the police were concerned, they were prime suspects and their illegal foray couldn't have come at a more opportune time. Stealing the eggs of birds of prey was treated as a very serious offence, as he had already told these two. A couple of scapegoats would come in *very* handy. He grinned again to himself.

The goshawks watched the trio of humans until they were out of sight. Then the birds took off from their perch and flew silently away.

Garn let Ka lead the way. Since the loss of her eggs she had been very disturbed, wherever she wanted to go, he would follow. He thought perhaps she would begin the search all over again, hunting every thicket in the hope that she might come upon her missing eggs.

Suddenly, though, she was much calmer, there was a positiveness about her flight, as if she knew just where she was going and wanted to get there in the quickest possible time.

Ka headed straight back to the larch tree and, without further ado, settled herself down on the empty nest.

Chapter Five

*T*he goshawks had fresh cause for alarm.

They were familiar with helicopters; even in the remoteness of their former home the occasional one had flown over. At close quarters it was a frightening experience, at a distance it was yet another cause for wariness.

They were used to low flying aircraft, seldom did a day pass without one screaming over Black Hill. But they were gone within seconds. Helicopters were different, they travelled slowly like some gigantic mechanical bird of prey methodically looking for a kill. Garn and Ka sped away the moment they heard one, sought safety in the thickest part of the forest, huddled in the firs until the great flying beast was no more than a drone in the distance. They never associated it with Man.

One bright sunny May morning no less than two helicopters appeared over Black Hill, flying much faster than they usually did, as if they had some specific destination and purpose in mind.

Garn prepared to take to the wing but his mate remained stubbornly on the nest. She was clearly frightened but she made no move to seek safety in flight. It was all very puzzling; had she been sitting eggs or rearing chicks he could have understood it, but the nest was empty. All the same, he remained by her side.

Garn regarded the flying monsters with apprehension. They would pass directly overhead, they could not fail to spot the hawks. What chance did Garn and Ka stand?

After some minutes Garn realized that the roaring noise wasn't getting any closer. If anything, it was quieter. Perhaps the creatures were planning to sneak up on their prey.

Then, the sound was fading. Garn turned, saw that both machines had changed course, they were skirting the southern side of the hill. He continued to watch until they were no more than tiny dots in the sky.

Doubtless they had not seen the goshawks. If they had, they would not have flown away.

Throughout the day other helicopters appeared at all too frequent intervals but, unbelievably, none flew over the wooded slope which was the goshawks' adopted domain.

There were other disturbances, too. Land Rovers and heavy trucks trundled along the narrow road past Pen-y-Cwm at the foot of Black Hill, vehicles which had been painted green and brown so that they matched the clothing of the drivers and those who sat hunched in the rear; some of the trucks carried up to a dozen men. But none turned up the rough track that led to the area once used by the woodcutters. Helicopters and vehicles were on the move all day long, going somewhere, then returning and starting all over again.

No movement, vehicular or human, was missed by the goshawks. When Man was present in numbers, it was extremely worrying. But only one man was in close proximity to the goshawks' larch tree, the tall forestry ranger, dressed similarly to those who travelled the road. He stood back in the trees, almost invisible.

Swift was even more alert than usual, not once did he relax his vigilance. Every few minutes he scanned the surrounding woodland through his binoculars and checked that Ka was still on the nest, noted Garn's whereabouts. But today Garn did not hunt, he sensed danger all around, hunger was a small price to pay for safety. This was no ordinary day on Black Hill, something was happening which presented yet another threat to the hawks' existence.

Towards mid-day Garn made a short reconnaissance, flew as far as the sheep fields. There were humans there, too, this time on foot. There seemed a lot of them, more than he had ever seen together at any one time. They were spread out, walking in a straggling line; some had dogs on leashes, powerful brutes that reminded him of wolves. They pulled, strained, it was as much as their handlers could do to hold them in check. The animals were scenting. *Hunting*!

Garn saw humans in Hopwas Wood and the Soldiers' Wood, too. There was something different about these, though, they lacked the arrogance of those out on the fields; they slunk through thick cover. Some hid and would not have been spotted except by a sharp-eyed hawk. They reminded Garn of rabbits cowering in the undergrowth. *Prey*!

On his homeward flight the goshawk spied men on Black Hill but for some reason, like the helicopters, they avoided the area around the larch tree. It was almost as though they had been forbidden to go near.

Only Swift, it seemed, was permitted to stray near the goshawks. He returned each morning to take up his solitary vigil and at dusk he was replaced by his younger companion.

Gone now was the tranquillity that had followed the cessation of chainsawing. Instead, there was the roar of helicopters, back and forth all the time, gigantic mechanical birds of prey scouring the surrounding countryside for victims. But they never came near the nest.

Garn was forced to hunt, for neither he nor Ka could go without food. He felled a fleeing woodpigeon, stripped it of its feathers and feasted ravenously. His next kill would be for Ka. She was as reluctant to leave the nest as she had been when she was sitting her eggs. He was curious but he did not question her reasons, his duty was to provide and protect.

Having satisfied his hunger, he flew on, passed over the watching ranger. It was then that he saw two men slinking through the trees. Garn flew silently up into a spruce, waited and watched. Up until now the humans had avoided the goshawks' domain; suddenly two of them were creeping into it. It boded ill for the birds.

In spite of the warmth the humans wore long coats that were torn and muddied, flapped at their ankles. Their boots had no laces and slopped on their feet. Their faces were blacked, blended with the gloom of the forest. They walked wearily, they paused to rest every few yards.

Possibly their vigilance was dulled by exhaustion; at any other time they might have noticed the ranger standing with his back against a tree trunk, but they were almost level with him when he suddenly stepped out in front of them.

"What d'you think you're doing here?" Swift's tone was as angry as his expression. "Don't you chaps know this area is out of bounds? You've got maps, haven't you?"

"We ain't doin' no harm," the one in the lead spoke wearily, wiped his forehead with his sleeve. "The dogs picked up our scent, the task force would've caught us if we hadn't dodged in here."

"Which is the whole point of the exercise," Swift sighed. "You move at night, cross open ground under cover of darkness. You're allowed to lie up in the forest by day but not in *here*. This is an exclusion zone."

"Yeah, we know," the fugitives hung their heads, "but *why*? What harm are we doin' here?"

"This is a conservation area and prohibited to both escaped prisoners-of-war, because that's what you're supposed to be, and the Hunter Force. Even helicopters aren't allowed to fly over it."

"You mean . . . we might disturb *birds* and the like?" the tired army recruit sneered.

"Exactly."

"That's crazy," the second rookie was astounded. "We're trainin' to be SAS. We have to dodge the pursuing force, we're put back in the ranks if we're captured. We ain't goin' to make a noise or disturb anything. And, anyway, even if we did frighten the birds, which is more important, mister, training up a force to defend this country if it gets invaded by an enemy or alarming a bloomin' hawk? Somebody's got their priorities wrong, if you ask me!"

"I ought to take you back to your Training Officer," Swift's tone had softened a fraction. "Civilians are asked to assist in the capture of the escaping force because that's what would happen if you were hiding out in a hostile country. But *my* priority is the protection of a rare nesting site which has already been robbed once this season. I guess you're not interested in that but it happens to be my job. Now, off you go, back the way you came, and don't let me catch sight of you in here again."

Garn watched the two men leave, dragging their feet in their tiredness. He did not understand, only that they had quarrelled with the ranger.

Garn flitted away. Shortly afterwards he killed a blackbird, flew straightaway with it back to the tall larch. As he alighted, Ka stood up, stretched her cramped wings.

It was then that Garn saw the three plain white eggs in the nest beneath her. So that was why his mate had stubbornly refused to leave the nest! It was late in the breeding season but Nature had given her a second chance to rear a brood.

There was still time.

Chapter Six

The human hunters and their skulking prey were long gone from the hills. The helicopters and trundling trucks were no longer seen, just those low flying aircraft but that was a daily routine to which the goshawks had become accustomed.

Only the forestry watcher remained, either Swift or his deputy or occasionally Reuben the gamekeeper. Nobody else came to Black Hill, its former tranquillity returned.

Three fluffy goshawk chicks hatched and soon Garn was hunting throughout all the daylight hours in order to meet the demand for food in the nest. But his task was not proving easy.

When the hawks had been released on Black Hill there had been rabbits in abundance; they were easy prey for an experienced predator. Then, with the onset of summer, there were fewer rabbits to be found in the forest. At first Garn was not aware that the numbers had decreased, so long as he caught a couple each day that was ample for his needs.

Early morning and late evening rabbits crept from their deep woodland warrens to graze the lush pastureland on the edge of the forest. Garn was now back to peak fitness and it was either a very swift or an extremely lucky rabbit which made it safely back to cover as he dived out of the sky.

The rabbits were more sluggish in their movements these days, even lethargic; Garn noticed this but it did not concern him. Those he killed had swollen eyes, they never even saw him coming. They squealed briefly when he struck. But as their flesh was as wholesome as it had always been, he gave the matter no further thought.

Until one day he found no rabbits at all and that was very strange, indeed. So he turned his attention to the wood-pigeons which used the vast conifer thickets as a roost.

Pigeon hunting was much more difficult these days now that the birds were aware that there was a rapacious killer in the area. Many of them had deserted the Black Hill for safer woodlands, Hopwas Wood and the Soldiers' Wood. Those that stayed were very wary, they scattered far and wide at Garn's approach, had learned that the approaching distant speck heralded sudden death.

The jays and magpies warned their feathered neighbours when Garn was in the vicinity. That machine gun-like chattering, the harsh screeching, sent songbirds fluttering into the nearest cover, only emerging when the goshawk had passed and all was safe.

Garn transferred his attention to mice and voles in the deep woods. It was hard and tedious work; it needed several kills and constant flights to and from the nest in order to satisfy the demands of his growing family.

He knew that he had to find a healthy colony of rabbits somewhere and that meant going further afield. There were surely still some rabbits on the grassland between Hopwas Wood and Badger Wood, he had seen them there that time when he and Ka had searched far and wide for the missing eggs. He knew that he must return there if he was to provide ample fresh meat for Ka and her fledglings.

Garn set off, flew low, followed the hedgerows as was his nature. There were sheep in nearly every field, stupid creatures that did nothing but graze and panicked at the slightest disturbance. A flock was huddled in a corner, bleating plaintively; the goshawk saw a man with a black dog which appeared to have the sheep cornered, darted to and fro whenever one tried to break away, drove it back. Garn didn't understand what was going on, he avoided that particular tract.

Crows were the bane of his life. Often a dozen or more of them appeared when jays or magpies shrieked, as if the birds had deliberately raised the alarm that a hawk was in the vicinity. Corvids never harmed Garn or Ka, they just made a nuisance of themselves once they spied them, wheeling and diving, mobbing them with raucous calls. It was a kind of game but it became very tiresome after a while. It ruined the hunting too for mammals, and other birds associated the continuous chorus with their dreaded enemy and took cover.

It was on a steep hillside below Hopwas Wood, a place where there was a larger sandy rabbit warren out in the open, that a corvid attracted Garn's attention. He was about to skirt the place before the bird saw him and called for its companions, but he hesitated because there was definitely something strange about it.

The other was trying to take off, flapping its huge wings, but all that it succeeded in doing was tumbling back and fluttering helplessly. As if, for some reason, it was unable to fly. Garn became even more curious; a crow at his mercy was of no interest to him because he had no inclination to mock and taunt. Possibly it had a broken wing. He decided to take a look, swooped in closer and landed.

He saw that the other was a raven, larger than a carrion crow, its call a deep-throated *cronk*. It leaped up again and when it fell back Garn saw that something was attached to its one leg, an iron implement that had a rusted chain secured to a stout peg in the ground. This time the black bird sprawled with outstretched wings, regarded Garn suspiciously.

The leg trapped by twin rows of closed jaws was bleeding; undoubtedly, it was also broken. Its wings beat feebly and there was despair and pain in the small fast-blinking eyes.

Garn felt a surge of pity for a natural enemy, doubtless whatever had befallen it was Man's doing. Close by were the remains of a dead rabbit, the bones picked clean of flesh, just the skeleton and a heap of torn fur.

The raven warned Garn not to remain around the sheep fields, they were a dangerous place. The farmers and shepherds hated both corvids and hawks, especially in the Spring when the lambs were born. Several times he had witnessed the death of an unsuspecting hawk or crow, killed with a stick that made a loud bang; the unfortunate bird fell from the sky, lay dead on the ground.

That was how it was around here; the raven's eyes reflected its pain. Man was your enemy, you had to be *very* cunning just to survive. He hunted the rabbits, trapped and snared them; the bird fluttered its wings again as if to demonstrate the extent of human cruelty. But most of the rabbits had died, lately they were to be seen crouched around the fields, blind and with swollen heads. That was Man's doing, too, for sure. But they were all gone now, for the foxes had cleared them, enjoyed an unprecedented harvest. The foxes would be starving without the rabbits, they'd probably start raiding the poultry farms and the game preserves and that would bring Man's wrath as never before upon all the other creatures in the countryside.

There had been the remains of one of those dead rabbits lying above the big warren. The raven was old and wise but his wisdom had temporarily deserted him. His curiosity had got the better of him, the rabbit wasn't set to a trap, he had seen that. But there had been a trap buried in the sandy soil close by and he had stepped right on to it . . .

It was the first time ever that Garn had felt sorry for a member of the corvid tribe. They had caused himself and Ka enough distress in the past, both here and in that other forest, sometimes following for hours; their din was deafening and the only chance was to elude them in the forest. But for the moment he forgave them, now all the creatures were united to elude Man's relentless efforts to kill them.

A dog yapped, a man shouted. That would be the farmer rounding up his sheep a couple of fields away. Perhaps it was the same man who had set this cruel trap. Why he should do that puzzled the goshawk. After all, corvids were *inedible*.

Garn could not remain here much longer, the farmer would be coming once he had finished with his sheep. Alas, there was no way in which the goshawk could help the raven for he wasn't strong enough to ease those powerful jaws of the trap apart. So, there was no point in staying here.

Garn was quickly airborne, following the downhill hedgerow in his customary low, darting flight, weaving between some blackthorn trees. Searching. Hunting.

The rabbit he found and killed was something of an anticlimax. The thrill of every hunt was in the chase, for the goshawk is not an ambusher like his relative, the buzzard. A rabbit on open ground will bolt for cover or hide in a tuft of grass. Sometimes it will escape unscathed.

Not this one. It was barely half-grown, perhaps its naivety was the reason it squatted motionless, frozen into immobility at the sight of a fearsome hawk hurtling down upon it.

Or, more likely, it was totally unaware of the pending attack, blinded and numbed into insensitivity so that the kill was a merciful coup-de-grace. Garn stood over it, saw the bulbous head, horribly swollen by the weeping sores that buried the eyes. For the second time that morning he experienced a strange sense of pity.

The goshawk had never before witnessed myxomatosis, its curse was unknown in the forests of Eurasia where rabbit populations never exploded to a point where disease must cull. Near-starving foxes and wolves ensure that does not happen during the long winters. A dead creature was rarely seen; Garn understood only that events here were determined by Man. And Man was becoming a threat to the goshawks existence as well as to that of every living creature which inhabited these wooded hills. And yet, it seemed that Man was also trying to protect the hawks. It was beyond comprehension.

Garn raked the rabbit's fur away, the flesh beneath was as succulent as any which he had tasted. He would have gorged himself there and then except that he remembered Ka and her growing brood. Their survival was more important than his own.

The dead rabbit was small and light enough to carry; he took off, clutching it in his talons, flying fast, zig-zagging. The farmer had finished with his sheep, he was walking towards the field where the raven fluttered in the trap, the dog following at his heels.

He looked up and saw the goshawk. His ash stick was uplifted, pointed in surprise. Garn weaved, jinked, every movement by Man was menacing. Had not the raven spoken of sticks that went bang and killed instantly? Swerving, accelerating the hawk skimmed a hedge and was lost from the man's view.

Soon Garn was back at the nest, delivering his catch to the cheeping, hungry fledglings.

At least Garn knew where there were a few rabbits to be found even if they did not offer sport and their heads were swollen and festered. They were food for a growing family of goshawks. The raven had been wrong, all the rabbits had not died.

The bloated rabbits were easy prey but the area was fraught with danger. Man must be outwitted. It was a challenge.

Tomorrow Garn would return to the fields for another rabbit.

Chapter Seven

There was no sign of the raven when Garn returned to the fields shortly after daybreak the following morning. The trap was gone, too. Or else it was cunningly concealed somewhere close by, waiting for its next victim. There was no way that Garn was alighting anywhere in the vicinity.

He flew in a cautious circle, checking to see if the farmer was anywhere about. There was no sign of him and the sheep were grazing peacefully, which they would not have been if that dog was around. Garn's thoughts returned to rabbits.

There were none to be seen. He hunted the hedgerows and the clumps of gorse; not so much as a stealthy movement caught his eye. It was uncanny, disturbing. There were always rabbits about at first light and dusk. Where were they?

They were all dead, victims of that terrible disease, it had wiped out the entire population of these fields and woods.

There were woodpigeons but they were wary, flying fast and giving the pastureland a wide berth as if they knew that the goshawk was now out here. Perhaps the jays and magpies had already spread the warning. In the wild word travelled fast.

Garn surprised a moorhen on an overgrown reed-fringed

pool, caught it before it had time to dive to safety below the algae-covered surface, swept it up in his talons in the manner of his distant relative, the osprey, that majestic sea hawk which took fish lying within its reach.

At least the goshawks would not go hungry today. Garn knew that tomorrow he must widen his hunting grounds even further.

A flock of crows spied him on his homeward flight, rose in a mass from a dead sheep which they had picked clean the previous day but had returned to optimistically. There was nothing left apart from the bones and fleece. Suddenly, the prospect of hawk-baiting was much more appealing.

Some more crows appeared from the next field where they had been foraging in a pile of farmyard manure, a black cloud of screeching scavengers with ragged wings. Garn checked, changed course. There were more corvids up ahead of him, they were all around.

Their diving and swooping had him shying; it was a familiar situation, they had never ever harmed him but there was always the fear that they might; they were so aggressive, so noisy, so frightening when you found yourself caught in the midst of them. Garn tried to take evasive action; wings fanned him, beaks snapped, he was buffeted by growled corvid insults. It was impossible to maintain a direct course.

His tormentors followed his every turn, his swiftness of flight was hampered by their very numbers. Even more crows joined the affray, the flapping swarm was growing by the minute.

Garn clutched the moorhen tightly, if he dropped it then victory would be theirs and the young goshawks would go hungry. But it meant that he was unable to use his talons to slash at his enemies.

This way, that way, his confusion led to a loss of direction. He had no idea now which way the tall larch tree lay.

Suddenly, the deafening affray was brought to an abrupt end. Two loud bangs checked the cawing; for a few seconds there was a shocked silence. Crows back-flapped, wheeled, scattered. Something thudded on to the springy grass – a crow, breast uppermost, wings outstretched. The gentle summer breeze ruffled its feathers. Otherwise it lay motionless. Dead.

A second crow planed down, landed awkwardly, flapped just once. Then it, too, rolled over and lay still.

The flock scattered, called angrily from a distance. They knew death when they saw it, they were only too familiar, too, with Man's sticks that banged and killed. Only their mischievous stupidity, their concentrated aggression towards a bird of prey, had enabled the human with the gun to creep along the hedge until he was within range of them.

The need for stealth gone, Reuben stood up to reload his shotgun. Two down, he had hoped for more with a double charge of scattershot fired into the thick of the flock. Crows were relentless egg hunters around the game preserves during the breeding season, sometimes they took pheasant chicks, too. Hawks were an even greater menace but the do-gooders had seen fit to protect them by law.

His fingers fumbled cartridges from his pocket. That goshawk was speeding away, he should have taken it first whilst the opportunity was there; crows could be killed at any time.

Too late! The hawk with the long tail and stubby wings had regained its composure, was flying fast and low in the opposite direction. The gun reloaded, Reuben fired after it but it was already out of range, his shots were but a gesture of his frustration. He stood and watched until the bird was out of sight. Maybe shooting it here in the open would have been a mistake, anyway, he consoled himself; you never knew who was watching you. Old Hughes, the farmer, might be only a couple of fields away, he was the sort who would report you even though he killed hawks and ravens in his rabbit traps.

Nevertheless, one had to be very careful. Reuben reloaded his gun a second time. Anybody witnessing his killing of the crows would applaud him for saving the goshawk and that couldn't be bad! And when the opportunity arose to shoot those goshawks nobody would even suspect him. Hadn't he volunteered to take a shift on the forestry's 'Hawk Watch' along with the rangers? Hadn't he apprehended a couple of youths on their way to shoot the birds and thrown suspicion of plundering the eggs on them? He'd heard that Ben and Ian had been released without charge due to lack of evidence. That was a pity but it couldn't be helped.

When the goshawks disappeared without trace, as they surely would before long, the foresters would come rushing to Reuben, the gamekeeper, to help search for the missing birds. And, who knows, the dead goshawks might just turn up in one of Farmer Hughes's fields . . .

Reuben's expression hardened, he had seen the havoc which a sparrowhawk could wreak in the game preserves. A goshawk was, in effect, a giant sparrowhawk. He could not afford to take any chances.

The rabbits were gone from the grassland around Hopwas Wood. Garn watched from the trees, both in the early morning and late evening, but there was not a single rabbit to be seen. If there had been any left alive they would most certainly have crept out to feed. The terrible disease had wiped out every one of them. The wise old raven had been proved right.

Garn watched a fox hunting the deserted pastureland. There was something strange about it. He had seen enough foxes to know how they hunted – stealthy movers that took advantage of any available cover, lay in wait for long periods in the hope of ambushing an unsuspecting victim. This one did none of these; it wandered almost aimlessly, sniffed here and there, seemed to lack cunning. There was no method to its movements. Eventually it just trotted away.

It was as though the whole countryside was changing and

it was disturbing to a hawk who relied on hunting for the survival of its species.

Garn had to find food somewhere. He killed voles and mice, a fat rat and a skylark that rose high into the air out of the tussocky grass and gave him a truly sporting strike. But that was small consolation for the tiny amount of meat which it offered.

The woodpigeons had moved on to the Soldiers' Wood beyond Hopwas Wood. This had nothing to do with Garn's presence, simply that there was a lush field of dazzling yellow oilseed rape close by which offered plentiful feeding.

Garn killed a second skylark; there had only been one resident pair on Black Hill this Spring. Their nest had been plundered by the crows and now there was no likelihood of this rapidly declining species gracing the hills with their distinctive trilling flight call.

Garn concentrated his efforts on sparrows and finches of which there were plenty. But, like the woodpigeons, they also became wary of his pillage and kept in thick cover where they were safe.

Garn knew that he was going to have to find another source of food very soon. The young goshawks were growing fast but until they were able to hunt for themselves they relied upon him.

He determined to extend his search even further.

Chapter Eight

Swift and Jackson, and sometimes Reuben, still came to Black Hill to keep watch on the goshawks' nest. Once the young were able to fly the danger would have lessened; right now they were vulnerable and a worthy prize for any unscrupulous trainer of falcons. They would fetch good money on the black market.

Swift watched their progress with interest through his binoculars. He looked forward to witnessing the fledglings' first flight; he would then be relieved of much responsibility and have more time for other duties. The tree felling would be able to continue, its cessation had cost the forestry a lot of money in compensating the contractors. Conservation was a costly matter, but Timpson was adamant that it was worth it for public relations.

It was on a hot Sunday afternoon that the ranger's worst fears were confirmed. He had been at his observation post since seven that morning when he had relieved a weary Jackson. Reuben had volunteered for the night watch but that was a few hours away yet. Swift didn't trust Reuben. The gamekeeper was no conservationist at heart, all he cared about were his hand-reared pheasants; he related them to his wages and generous tips from wealthy sportsmen on shooting days. There were rumours about Reuben, whispers of badger digging. But there was no proof. All the same, the forestry ranger believed in that old adage about there being no smoke without fire. Timpson regarded the gamekeeper as a useful ally in the forest and that was all there was to it.

Swift jerked out of his drowsiness, was instantly alert. He heard a vehicle coming up the steep narrow lane from the main road below; its engine laboured, the gears grated. He caught a glimpse of bright orange between the trees. It faltered and he heard it turning off the hard surface on to the rutted forest road, struggling in bottom gear.

Swift grimaced, stepped out on to the track and waited. Public access was permitted by the forest authorities; vehicular access was forbidden.

An orange minibus rumbled into view round the bend, its tyres spinning in the soft ground. The driver revved, slowed when he saw that somebody barred his way. Heads bobbed behind him, faces stared with expressions of amazement at seeing another human being in this remote place.

The minibus came to a halt, its engine ticking over uncertainly. Then it stalled.

"Can I help you?" Swift's tone was polite but firm, a veiled reprimand to the driver and his passengers.

"We've come to look at the goshawks," the man behind the wheel was heavily bearded, there was a hint of aggression in his voice.

"What goshawks?" The ranger spoke guardedly, unfortunately the theft of the eggs had been well publicised, even localised.

"The ones that had their eggs stolen. They're somewhere around here," the driver produced a pamphlet, flipped the pages. "Here, see for yourself. Nesting site on Black Hill, close to the Cwm road. Where that cross is marked."

Swift's expression was angry as he looked at the page which the driver held up. It was headed 'Rare Nesting Sites of the Borderlands'. "Where did you get this?"

48

"They're free to the bird watching society, the subscriptions cover 'em. Why?"

The ranger took a deep breath to steady himself. Rare birds' eggs were stolen because people were told where the nests were; secrecy would have prevented half the thefts. But somebody made money out of selling site maps to bird watchers; just as the thieves made money out of the sale of stolen eggs and the forestry benefited from creating an image of conservation. The birdlife of these vast woods were the real losers, they were the puppets in Man's game, manipulated for a lot of reasons.

"You're not allowed to bring vehicles into the forest," Swift's tone was expressionless, diplomacy when dealing with members of the public was part of his training. You never showed your anger, except towards egg thieves and poachers.

"Please yourself, mate," the driver shrugged his shoulders. "I'll park down on the road at the bottom, we'll walk the rest of the way."

"This is an exclusion area."

"Who for?" The other's tone was rebellious.

"The public in general."

"Hang about!" The driver's cheeks flushed. "I got another leaflet here that says that there's public access to all forestry woodlands."

"That's right, but you have to keep to the designated rights of way and bridle paths. This track is not a right of way, it's used for forestry workers and contractors."

"Who says?" The occupants of the minibus were disembarking, a motley array of multi-coloured T-shirts and matching baseball caps. Each one carried either a pair of binoculars or a camera. A fair-haired young lady in shorts clutched a well worn copy of 'A Complete Illustrated Guide to the Birds of Great Britain'.

"It's my job, I'm a forest ranger," Swift spoke softly. "Nobody comes past me. Now, please drive back down to the road. The public right of way to Black Hill is on the

49

opposite side, you just follow the road right round, you can't miss it."

"But there aren't any goshawks *there*!" It was the lady who complained this time. "The forests belong to the public, we've a right to go anywhere we please. You can't stop us watching the goshawks."

Swift sighed, it was the popular misconceived argument which he had heard many times before. These people knew where the goshawks were, they were determined to see them. Again he resorted to diplomacy. "Tell you what, if I take you to where you can see the goshawks, will you promise me that you'll go away and not create any further disturbance."

They promised. The opportunity to be taken to a rare nesting site was too good to be true; all too often they tramped through acres of rough terrain where their booklet promised a nest and never found it.

Today was their lucky day.

The young goshawks were learning to fly. It was a traumatic experience, swaying precariously in the upper boughs of that huge larch tree, spreading their wings yet not having the confidence to launch themselves into the air. Their cajoling parents were becoming angry, shrieking at them.

Fal, the only cock amongst the trio and the smallest of the young, proved to be the bravest. He jumped, spread his wings, glided and made a somewhat clumsy landing on a pine branch opposite. Jek and Li, his sisters, watched in awe, launched themselves after him as Ka edged threateningly towards them. Jek made it, Li fluttered down to the ground below, made a soft landing in some bracken and proceeded to squawk her dismay.

Garn and Ka ignored her, kept a wary eye out for any vermin that might approach. Sheer desperation would be her salvation, it was best that she made it back up to the nest on her own. She did this in gradual stages, fluttering from bough to bough, until finally all five goshawks perched proudly outside the nest. The first lesson had been successful.

The young birds' powers of flight progressed daily until at last they were all wheeling over the forest, calling loudly. *Ca-ca-ca . . . gek-gek-gek*. The chicks had now become fledglings, grown to the size of a sparrowhawk. Their blunt wings were capable of strong flight, their eyestripe had turned white, but only when the vertical markings on their breasts became horizontal would they be truly mature.

Swift decided that the long hours spent watching over the goshawks were no longer necessary. The project had been successful, they had reared their young at the second attempt. They were able to fend for themselves. Until the next breeding season came round.

Garn and Ka's next task was to teach their brood to hunt. There were no rabbits, woodpigeons were too big and swift for the young, so they began their lessons with small birds. A nearby field of ripening corn had attracted flocks of sparrows; these were relatively easy prey in the beginning, the only problem being that the young goshawks had difficulty in deciding which bird to strike down amidst so many. Often they changed their minds in full flight and indecision resulted in a fruitless hunt, all the sparrows scattering and hiding in a thick hedgerow for the next few hours.

But the goshawks learned by their mistakes and for a time they were feeding themselves on the sparrows they caught. There were finches, too, and blackbirds and thrushes. None were spared their predations.

Before long that corn field was almost devoid of birdlife, those that had not perished at the vicious talons had sought safer places; farmyards with poultry offered gleanings and Man's protection. The big hawks kept well clear of human habitation.

So far.

Once again prey was becoming scarce. And there was

another reason for moving on from the area in close proximity to the larch tree that was their home. No longer did Man keep a day and night watch and within a week humans were infiltrating those woodlands.

Another minibus full of passengers arrived and this time there was nobody to guide them to a place where they could observe unobtrusively; they were not content to wait patiently and watch from a distance. There was no sign of the goshawks, they must surely be hiding in that high nest.

The crowd gathered at the foot of the tree, shouted and clapped their hands. Nothing stirred above them so they threw stones and sticks. Still no head peered over the platform of interwoven twigs.

A man in shorts and heavy walking boots boasted of his mountaineering exploits, a larch tree was no problem. The others gazed in awe as he climbed steadily, gasped when a branch broke but he quickly grabbed another. Up and up, until finally he was straddling the bough that held the nest, looking into it and shaking his head in disappointment. A thumbs-down signal told the watchers on the ground that the nest was empty.

The birds had flown, they did not need the nest any longer. After such a mammoth climb it was a shame to return empty-handed; the man began to dismantle the structure, tearing at it, throwing it down to his laughing audience. There were some feathers adhering to the moss lining, enough for everybody to go home with a souvenir.

The humans did not see any wrong in their act of vandalism; the goshawks had no further use for the nest. They could build another next Spring.

Others trespassed to the site now that it was unguarded. The tree was scaled several times, a set of initials were crudely carved in the bark.

Reuben came at dusk one evening, his customary shotgun cradled under his arm. His practised eye read what had happened as another might have read a newspaper. The 'amateurs' had been and desecrated, no goshawk had been harmed. His anger was directed at the bungling of those who did not understand the countryside; they had driven the goshawks away, the birds would be much more elusive from now on.

Reuben had no idea where they had gone but one thing was certain, their plundering would increase as the young birds grew and learned to kill, their need for fresh meat would be increased.

No small birds or animals would be safe on Black Hill or in Hopwas Wood. Reuben's hand-reared pheasants had only last week been transferred to the big release pen, they would be vulnerable to attack from the air.

Never before had such danger threatened the game preserves. Reuben would not rest until the threat to his pheasants was removed.

Garn had left Ka instructing their family in the art of hunting and flown on further than he had ever been before. He flew parallel to the main road then cut into Hopwas Wood by the big white house. Further on he came upon the fenced mound that was an underground reservoir, an area devoid of trees where the woodpigeons flighted mornings and evenings. And still he saw no rabbits.

It was beyond the reservoir, amidst the tall pines, that he found the large open-topped pen. Constructed of strong wire netting, its roughly rectangular shape enclosed almost a hectare. Around its perimeter was an electric fence to keep out prowling foxes.

Garn alighted on a branch and stared in disbelief at the scene which greeted him inside the release pen. Never before in his life had he seen so many pheasants, he never guessed that such numbers existed!

The birds scratched and pecked at scattered corn, few of them had tail feathers, many were badly pecked, an infectious habit amongst pheasants kept in captivity for any length of time. Some had strange, inexplicable brightly coloured attachments on their beaks, most had brails or pinions to prevent them from flying out of the pen. They cheeped constantly; a fully grown cock in mature red and golden plumage called loudly. This was his domain, the younger males kept well out of his way. It was a life of boredom but the pheasants hatched in the Spring had known nothing else, beyond their confines they would have been easy prey for foxes and other predators.

Garn watched in silence. For weeks he had struggled to find food for his family; here there was more than enough, penned in readiness for him.

He swooped, killed a young hen pheasant, scattered the rest. He fed leisurely and then started out on the long flight home. Tomorrow he would lead Ka and their young here for this surely was a land of plenty.

The goshawks had found their Utopia.

Part Two

DESTRUCTION

Chapter Nine

The area of Hopwas Wood in which the goshawks made their new home was amidst the Scots pines between the large white house and the covered reservoir. It was much less remote than Black Hill, barely half a mile from the village, but its advantages were considerable.

It was within easy striking distance of the penned pheasants and there were enough birds in that enclosure to feed the hawks for a very long time. There was more human activity around, certainly, for children played on the edge of the wood on fine evenings after school but they did not climb the trees; they built a tree house on a low branch and that occupied them fully. They laughed and shouted but their chatter was harmless. They were not interested in wild creatures.

People walked and exercised their dogs in the wood but the animals did not *hunt*. Mostly the dogs were kept at heel, or on leashes, for this was Reuben's domain and he did not tolerate unruly pets.

The disturbance was negligible compared to the breeding season on Black Hill. The humans were totally oblivious of the goshawks' presence; the hawks watched them unseen from the dense pine branches. Garn and Ka had taught their offspring the importance of stealth; they flew silently, killed swiftly and noiselessly, and kept out of sight.

Fal and Jek and Li were almost old enough to leave their parents. Summer was waning and if the young hawks made no move to leave soon then their parents would drive them away. Self-reliance was important to the survival of every species in the wild, Nature decreed that it must be so. This was Garn and Ka's territory, the brood they had raised must stake a claim of their own elsewhere. But for another week or two they would all stay together.

The large garden of the white house was very overgrown, it had not been tended for some time. The extensive shrubberies provided roosting for Great Tits with their song that was like a saw being sharpened, hordes of sparrows and starlings. And there was a bird table littered with all manner of thrown-out household food.

A man shambled out of the house most mornings, added to the morass of food on the table; sometimes he scraped plates on to it. The goshawks observed all the activities in this garden from a high tree where it bordered the wood. It seemed that this human's main interest in life was feeding the wildlife; grey squirrels climbed up to feast on the soggy offerings and when they had satisfied themselves and departed, small birds came in numbers.

The man spent a lot of time watching from a window that overlooked this messy feeding place; sometimes there was a bright flash that temporarily scattered the birds. On occasions a grey-haired woman joined him but she never came outside.

There was an overgrown pond, too. Once there had been goldfish in it but a sharp-eyed heron passing over had spied them. They were easy prey. Very occasionally the heron returned to check if the pool had been re-stocked but it had not been back since the early Spring when some frogspawn had hatched.

For the moment the pheasants in the release pen were

forgotten for this garden offered a wealth of sport to the goshawks. They confined their hunting to daybreak; the occupants of the house were rarely seen before mid-morning.

The resident family of grey squirrels were decimated within the first couple of days which meant that the birds using the table became braver. Once a dozen tits were all feeding together; five were taken before the rest fled to the safety of a spreading laurel.

A rhododendron shrubbery was inhabited by a colony of starlings that had opted for an easy lifestyle. These speckled greedy birds were a nuisance; they drove many of the other species away from the bird table. The goshawks did not trouble them, starlings were a last resort when nothing else was left.

The daily tally mounted; there were only three tits left, the sparrows were reduced to single numbers, too. Much to the goshawks' chagrin, a sparrowhawk showed up one day; perhaps it knew about the garden and visited it spasmodically between hunting the hedgerows in the fields. It caught sight of Fal and left hurriedly. It did not return.

The man was clearly concerned at the absence of birds; he deposited a whole loaf of sliced bread on the rickety shelf and retired to his usual place at the window to watch. The woman joined him and they remained there for some considerable time but only starlings flew down to feed.

The goshawks remained out of sight in their tree.

The next day the man appeared with a companion. Garn recognized him instantly, it was Reuben. The gamekeeper examined the ground beneath the bird table, held up some feathers. He turned, pointed to the wood beyond the garden, made a swooping movement with his hand. The man nodded as if he understood and they both went back indoors.

Garn and Ka had the feeling that the garden might no longer be a safe place for them. It was time to return to the pheasant pen.

It was time too for Fal, Jek and Li to be going their own way. They might have lingered a while longer with their parents but Garn and Ka were not prepared to tolerate them.

The adult hawks became aggressive, confronted the younger ones with flapping wings, hissed threateningly. The trio of immature birds backed away along a branch. Li flew to another tree and watched in hurt amazement; Jek followed her; only Fal stood his ground. A talon slashed at him, he lost his balance, opened his wings and fluttered away.

The young goshawks kept their distance; instinctively they understood what was expected of them but had hoped, perhaps, that it would never happen. Strangers in a strange land, they had none of their own kind to join up with. Sparrowhawks and buzzards were more fortunate in that respect.

Garn took to the wing and, followed by Ka, flew over the treetops in a wide circle, dropping back on to the same bough; a territorial gesture. The young birds must go and find a place of their own for their survival depended upon their own ability to outwit humans and kill for food. The adult birds would protect them no longer.

It was some time before they left. Fal went first, flew a couple of hundred yards before alighting; the two females joined him. They did not look back, they understood. They would explore the big wood in stages until they found somewhere to their liking.

The pheasant pen was an irresistible temptation. They perched, watched the birds scratching around for strewn grain. On the previous day Reuben and his assistant, Vinny, had worked hard, catching up each one and removing the artificial attachments which had been fixed to their beaks to prevent them from pecking one another in captivity. They removed, too, the pinions fastened on their wings. The pheasants were now able to fly unfettered even though their wings needed to strengthen; a few had already fluttered over the high mesh fence and were walking around the perimeter

trying to work out how to get back inside. There were tap-
ered wire funnels at intervals through which they could
squeeze once their limited intelligence had associated these
with a means of re-entry. By this method they were gradually
introduced to the life they would lead outside in the wood.
They would learn that it was safer to roost up trees than on
the ground where they were vulnerable to foxes. But there
was no safeguard against winged predators.

Fal swooped; he caught an unsuspecting hen pheasant
outside the fence. Death was instantaneous; the birds inside
the enclosure did not appear to have noticed. Jek and Li
joined him and they feasted with a newly-found satisfaction.
They could manage without their parents all right.

The pine wood beyond the pen stretched right up to that
area of dense rhododendrons which had once been the home
of the Hopwas badgers, a place where the starling flocks that
came from Russia wintered and fouled the vegetation. It
seemed an ideal habitat for the immature goshawks. For the
moment, anyway.

They roosted there on their first night away from their
parents, secure in the knowledge that there would be a pheasant for breakfast the next morning. Suddenly, independence
and freedom were an exciting prospect.

Reuben found the remains of the pheasant when he arrived
at the pen just after daybreak. He knelt and examined the
kill. The mode of slaughter was that of a sparrowhawk,
the fatal neck wound, the feathering of the carcass with
raking talons – except that a sparrowhawk would not have
stripped the bones of a three-quarter grown bird of almost
every morsel of flesh.

His keen eyesight differentiated between the claw marks
of pheasants and those of hawks in the soft ground; the
prints were too large for a sparrowhawk, certainly not those
of a buzzard. His expression was grim, he understood only
too well.

61

The gamekeeper carried his gun at all times, for he could come upon predators when he least expected them. The pheasants inside the enclosure were clamouring at the wire, they had long associated Reuben's arrival with generous scatterings of wheat. For the moment, though, he ignored them. He stepped back under a tree, stood motionless with his gun at the ready. It was only a matter of time.

The first rays of the morning sun slanted down through the overhead branches. A pigeon *cooed* contentedly and then took off suddenly, a frantic clattering of wings that was not its normal mode of flight out to feed in the fields. Something had scared it.

A jay screeched harshly, insistently, from a conifer thicket; a magpie chattered not far away. The guardians of the wood were not warning the other birds of the gamekeeper's presence, such calls would have more of a routine note to them. *These* warned of dire peril.

A goshawk landed in a tree twenty yards away; Reuben had neither heard nor seen its approach. It was not aware of him, it had eyes only for the milling pheasants inside the wire.

In a strange way the gamekeeper regretted the ease with which it offered itself as a target. Rather would he have had a quick snap shot through the trees, a clean and skilful kill. Fleetingly, he recalled that time when he had shot an escaped mongoose in such a manner one moonlight night. But marksmanship was of secondary consideration, the hawk was a threat to his charges, his job; he simply wanted it dead.

He eased the gun to his shoulder and pressed the trigger. The goshawk plummeted to the ground, wings closed. Even as Reuben lowered his gun, something dived from an upper branch, swerved and jinked with the speed of a woodcock and was lost from view before he could bring his barrels to bear upon it.

His reaction was one of mingled satisfaction and disappointment, he'd got one, with luck he might have had the pair. But the other would undoubtedly return.

He glanced about him furtively, guilt was an emotion unknown to Reuben. There was nobody in sight, but one never knew where those forestry rangers were, they roamed these woods at will.

Reuben worked quickly. There was a spade kept in the undergrowth by the pen door in readiness for any pheasant casualties that needed to be buried. He dug a hole in the sandy soil, examined the corpse before he dropped it in. A female; it was one hatched this year, the vertical breast markings were proof of that.

Reuben was thoughtful as he filled in the small grave. The late hatched goshawks had left their parents, moved to Hopwas Wood. There were two others at large, then. And the adults, of course, but there was no way of knowing where they were.

In the meantime the pheasants were vulnerable, he would have to take it in turns with Vinny mounting an armed guard throughout the hours of daylight. Buzzards and sparrowhawks they could cope with, goshawks meant death to every winged creature from tits to fully grown pheasants. Nothing was safe, their reintroduction to Britain after an eighty year absence was misguided conservation. Swift thought that way, too, but the ranger daren't voice his opinions because his job was at stake. And Swift would report you if he caught you killing one.

Reuben blamed himself. He should have put paid to the goshawks when he had the chance, nicking the first lot of eggs had only delayed the problem. But it still wasn't too late, the three young 'uns would've stayed together and the other two would come to the pheasants. That only left the old birds . . .

Chapter Ten

*F*al knew that the loud bang had killed Jek, he had been perched a few branches above her when she had tumbled lifeless to the ground. Only sheer speed had saved himself from a similar fate.

Li had been several trees away, she had followed him in his panic-stricken flight to safety. They had sped on past the wood which adjoined the rhododendrons, across the area of scrub and silver birch and over the grassland beyond. Until finally they arrived at the Soldiers' Wood. Here they rested in a stunted oak tree, bemused and frightened.

Why had their parents chased them away? If they had been allowed to stay in the wood close to the big white house then Jek would still be alive.

Close by a square of frayed red material fluttered in the wind on a tall post. The goshawk eyed it suspiciously; was this some new and terrible danger which they did not understand?

Underneath it was a board with red lettering on a white background. That, too, looked ominous. KEEP OUT. WAR DEPARTMENT. WHEN RED FLAG IS FLYING, FIRING IS IN PROGRESS.

The notice was old, some of the paint had flaked, but its warning was as dire today as it had been twenty years ago.

A sudden bang shattered the tranquillity of an overcast late summer morning. Li started, almost lost her footing on the branch. Fal clung on tightly with his talons. That was the same noise that had killed Jek!

Another bang, followed by several more, then a long volley that echoed and rolled across the surrounding hills. A flock of rooks hunting for wireworms rose off the newly-ploughed field alongside the wood. They cawed their protest, wheeled, then settled again to continue their hunt.

The next battue of rifle fire did not even alarm them. Quite clearly they were used to the noise once it started, only the first salvo had startled them.

Fal watched the rooks scratching and pecking. If they were unconcerned then he would follow their example. His composure was some comfort to Li. She would remain or fly off, whichever Fal chose to do.

They stayed.

There were only starlings left now in the untidy garden of the white house, those other visitors which had not fallen prey to the goshawks had fled to a safer place. Garn knew that the pheasants were the only source of food left; this time Ka would accompany him to the pen, she was able to kill her own prey outside the breeding season.

The flight took no more than a couple of minutes, the hawks travelled at an incredible speed. It seemed that no sooner had they dived from their perch above the garden than they were settling on a bough that overhung the release pen.

It was a moment to savour, Garn was in no hurry. They must single out their intended prey then launch themselves like feathered arrows of death.

Vinny, the assistant gamekeeper, was overweight and given

to laziness. The prospect of sitting by the release pen looking out for goshawks had a greater appeal to him than the routine chores which Reuben would otherwise have assigned him.

He took the .22 rifle out of the steel cabinet in the game-keeper's cottage and fitted the cylindrical silencer to the barrel as Reuben had instructed. The other words echoed in his brain, "take the rifle and the silencer so that nobody hears you shoot. And keep a lookout for folks as well as hawks. You never know where Swift is, 'e's like a bloomin' spook flittin' through them woods. And when you've shot a goshawk bury it *quick*!"

The task was doubly nerve-wracking after Reuben's warnings. Nobody would be up by the big pen, would they? In all probability the goshawks wouldn't put in an appearance, either, so Vinny could have a nice relaxing time, maybe even forty winks at lunchtime. He checked that he had his sandwiches and his flask. He was really going to enjoy himself today.

It was pleasantly warm in the woods but the late summer flies were troublesome. Vinny broke off a fern and swatted at them.

The pheasants scratched and pecked inside the mesh enclosure. Those that had flown over the top were frantically trying to find a way back in. Stupid birds!

He loaded the rifle, laid it on the ground beside him. It was going to be a long day but why should he worry, he was getting paid for it!

Reuben had an obsession with hawks and not a nice one. He was like the old time gamekeepers, his motto was 'If it's got a hooked beak – kill it!' Well, you couldn't legally shoot birds of prey in this enlightened age, and that was why Reuben had delegated the job to his assistant. 'If you get caught, Vinny, I never told you to shoot a gos.' Well, he hadn't exactly put it into words but that was what he meant. Reuben claimed to have *seen* goshawks round the pen, more likely he'd already shot one of them. He'd never admit it, not even to his best mate. Not that Reuben had any mates, just acquaintances.

It was a pound to a penny, Vinny made a bet with himself, that it was Reuben who had stolen those goshawk eggs and hoped that those two youths from the village would panic and confess. They hadn't. Good for them!

You couldn't trust Reuben.

A jay squawked and Vinny stiffened, his hand stretched out and rested on the rifle at his side. He heard some woodpigeons clattering out of the trees. Something was definitely on the mooch. He hoped it was just a fox.

All went quiet again. Whatever it was, it seemed to have gone away.

The pheasants inside the pen were crowded beneath the piles of branches which Reuben and Vinny had cut and thrown in to give them cover from sparrowhawks and buzzards. That had been hard work, just thinking about it made Vinny feel tired. The birds sensed danger of some kind. A couple outside the wire were running backwards and forwards, frantically trying to find an entrance. It always took the birds ages to realize what those tunnels were for.

Vinny listened again but the only sound was the far mewing of a soaring buzzard, it was probably over the Soldiers' Wood.

He saw a swift movement out of the corner of his eye; a large bird, a pair of stubby wings folded as it alighted out of his sight in the trees to his left. His pulses quickened, his mouth went suddenly dry. A goshawk had arrived.

He wondered what was the best thing to do. The bird had settled where he couldn't see it; it might stay there for hours until it had singled out its intended prey. Then it would pounce swiftly. Even then, it might kill where he didn't have a clear view of it in the middle of the debris of branches; as soon as it heard him move it would streak away. With the rifle he needed a sitting shot.

Reuben would be furious if a pheasant was killed and the goshawks escaped. There was only one thing for it, Vinny licked his lips nervously, he would have to try to stalk the predator before it struck.

He rose to his feet very slowly. He had often stalked foxes and rabbits, it was an art perfected by members of his profession. Lately, though, foxes seemed to be very much easier to creep up on, they weren't nearly so alert as they used to be, which was very strange indeed. You moved ever so slowly, tested the ground ahead of you with your foot before you put your full weight on it so that you didn't crack a dead twig; you used every vestige of cover available and, above all, you kept your head down and didn't look up. The paleness of a human face stood out starkly in natural surroundings. Another thing, creatures of the wild seemed to possess an uncanny sense of telepathy, they knew if you stared at them.

Vinny made it to the next tree. He waited again. Everywhere was unnaturally silent as though every inhabitant of Hopwas Wood was listening. The pair of pheasants had stopped their incessant running to and fro, they were hunched on the ground. The jay wasn't screeching any longer.

He moved forward again, it seemed an eternity before he reached the second tree, his hands were slippery on the rifle barrel. Unless he was mistaken, the goshawk had landed in that big oak tree twenty yards away; hesitantly, he risked a peep.

Yes, there it was!

Vinny lifted the rifle slowly to his shoulder, the barrel was shaking so much that it was almost impossible to take a sighting although the bird was clearly perched on a branch. It was the easiest target he'd ever been offered and he had the bonus of a telescopic sight to ensure that he did not miss. He took a deep breath in an attempt to regain his composure.

The barrel steadied, he lined the cross of the sight on the goshawk's barred breast, began to take a careful trigger pressure. And then, without warning, there was a crashing in the undergrowth behind him. In that moment of alarm and distraction, Garn dived, swerved out of sight behind the tree trunk in the same movement. Vinny had a fleeting glimpse of a second goshawk following in the wake of the first.

Somebody was coming, striding through the bracken with no regard for stealth; dead twigs cracked under his boots like pistol shots.

Vinny was both frightened and angry. Another second and the goshawk would have tumbled lifeless from its perch and he would have been caught red-handed. As it was, a golden opportunity to slay the nemesis of the pheasants was lost. That was the lesser of the two evils.

"Oh, it's you, Vinny!"

Vinny swallowed, unlike Reuben he experienced guilt. There was no mistaking the tall lean man who strode up to him.

It was Swift, the forestry ranger.

"There's . . . we've been 'avin' trouble with grey squirrels eatin' the pheasants' corn," the lie came clumsily and Vinny's face was red. "Reuben said to shoot 'em," he tapped the rifle as if that was proof of a legitimate foray.

"That's fine," the other's expression was stoic. "We want the squirrels thinned out, they do a lot of damage to the young trees. The squirrels appear to have had a very successful breeding season, worse luck. By the way, did you see that pair of goshawks take off from that tree over there?"

"No," Vinny's blurted lie was far from convincing. "I 'aven't caught sight of one since we were guardin' the nest."

"I wondered where they'd got to, I haven't seen them lately," Swift watched the other closely. "The chap who lives in the big house," he jerked a thumb in the direction of the main road, "rang up to complain that goshawks had decimated his little nature reserve of virtually every small bird.

Understandably, he was quite upset about it. Anyway, from what he told me I thought that the gosses had to be down this end and I was right. Of course, neither yourself nor Reuben would harm them, would you?"

"No . . . no, of course not," Vinny stammered.

"You'll just have to tolerate them," Swift snapped. "They'll maybe take the odd pheasant but they won't make any difference to your rearing programme in the long run."

"We could stretch some fishin' line across the top of the pen, it'd be almost invisible, then when they swooped . . ."

"*No!*" Swift almost shouted. "If you do that, and one gets killed, even if you didn't intend to kill it, you'll be fined heavily. You can't do anything that might harm them. Nor are you allowed to discourage them from a place they've chosen as a habitat by dismantling a nest or using bird scarers. Same with bats, if they take up residence in your bedroom, you're not allowed to shift 'em, you just have to put up with 'em."

"It's crazy."

"Yes, but I'm afraid it's the law and you have to obey it. My job is to see that the law is obeyed on forestry land. Remind Reuben of that when you next see him, please."

Vinny stood and watched the ranger stride away. There was no way of knowing how much Swift knew or guessed. But one thing was for sure, it was too risky to kill the goshawks here. All the same, he could not envisage Reuben tolerating them and that made him decidedly uneasy.

Garn and Ka sensed the danger in Hopwas Wood. Their survival instincts warned them that it was not safe to remain here. When they had fled at the ranger's approach they had seen the other man and he had been very close to them. He had meant them harm.

This part of the wood was too close to human habitation. In the beginning that had been convenient but now that they had slain most of the small birds there was no reason to stay. Only the pheasants were left and their preserve was too risky to hunt.

It was time to seek somewhere as far away from humans as possible.

Chapter Eleven

Fal and Li were not finding life easy without their parents. The young goshawks had not yet fully developed their hunting skills, they lacked experience. But even had they got that vital experience, there were no rabbits; the woodpigeons were very wary and kept well away from them. The small bird population had declined due to Garn and Ka's intensive slaughter.

Fal and Li concentrated their efforts on the pastureland, keeping well clear of farmers and shepherds, and survived on a meagre diet of mice and voles and the occasional finch. Carrion was something which they had not yet resorted to.

Except in the lambing season dead sheep were a rarity; goshawks, sparrowhawks and kestrels lived on their own freshly killed prey. Only buzzards and owls scavenged.

One day the goshawks spied the remnants of a buzzard-picked ewe below the Soldiers' Wood. The crows were still busy with the wireworms on the ploughed field, they did not even have time to mob the buzzards which had been attracted to the dead sheep.

The goshawks were hungry and those buzzards appeared to be feeding well. The larger birds retreated lazily at the approach of Fal and Li, flapped up from their feast; they seemed too bloated to fly far. Two settled on the nearest hedge, the third attempted to join its companions on the hawthorn but fluttered down on to the grass field. It hunched, squatted there. It was tired, it had difficulty in keeping its eyes open to watch the newcomers.

The two birds on the hedge swayed precariously, one grabbed a branch with its talons as it almost fell off. They blinked slowly, closed their eyes, opened them again with difficulty. Perhaps the warm sun added to their drowsiness. But the goshawks' only interest was in food, they had no interest in their larger relatives.

The meat gave off a rotting stench; it was crawling with maggots. It tasted bad, too. Fal swallowed a beakful. Had there been a fresh alternative he would have left this ewe to the maggots and scavengers, but his hunger dominated and he ripped at the flesh.

The goshawks ate until they could eat no more. Then they prepared to fly off; they stretched their wings but it was as if their bodies were too heavy to become airborne. They walked unsteadily, stood; squatted, huddled like the buzzards. All they wanted to do was to go to sleep.

They lost the urge to fly. In a way, it was very pleasant just squatting here; they relaxed in a way which they had never done before. They had eaten, their hunger was satisfied, there was no urgency to hunt and scour the countryside for food. They were in no danger, the buzzards on the hedge would be the first to spot anything that was a threat to them; the moment those huge wings opened, the goshawks would take off. At least, that was their intention.

The buzzard on the ground was lying down, wings still folded. That, truly, was a strange position in which to sleep. Fal thought it was very odd for the big hawks, like themselves, roosted in tall trees. Still, it was no business of his.

Li moved close to Fal, she sensed a need for companionship. Her vision was a little blurred; she too was curious about the prone buzzard. But if it had eaten as much as she had it was no wonder that it just wanted to sleep.

The goshawks gave up trying to keep their eyes open; their bodies sank lower; they used their wings to prop themselves up. Their heads drooped forward.

They heard the crows coming, the harsh calling turning to a more aggressive note as the corvids spied the hawks. Li flinched, pressed even closer against Fal as wingbeats ruffled her feathers. She tensed, anticipating an attack, forced her eyes open. It was almost dark, she could barely discern the silhouettes of the latest arrivals against a dusk sky.

But the crows were more interested in that dead sheep, wireworms were a delicacy rather than a sustaining meal. They landed, quarrelled noisily over the rotting flesh. Then they, too, fell silent.

Fal struggled to throw off his sleepiness. It was almost night and he and Li ought to be leaving, winging their way back to the safety of the Soldiers' Wood. He strained to open his wings, it was as though they were pinioned. That was when he first became afraid.

He could not keep his eyes open, but he had seen enough to alarm him. The crows had not left, either. They had feasted and stayed, a couple lay on the carcass, heads hanging limply over the side. They were sound asleep, as was the one which had rolled off and lay breast uppermost. Several more were perched on the ground around, heads bowed. Fal thought he could see others some distance away, some were standing dozing, others had keeled over.

What was happening? Why were these other birds unable to fly away, too?

Li was leaning her full weight against him; he braced himself or else she would have pushed him over. He could feel her breathing faintly. They had to get away from here before it was too late.

He did not have the strength, flight was an impossibility. If he couldn't fly, then he must find somewhere to hide. He moved, felt his mate slide from him, forced his eyes open and saw her lying on the ground. Her eyes did not open, not so much as a flicker. The breeze ruffled her plumage; she continued to lie there.

Now it was difficult to stand. Fal swayed one way, then the other. He took an unsteady step, only his talons digging into the turf kept him upright. The effort exhausted him, he waited. Breathing wasn't easy, either, each breath so shallow that he had to force it, gulp air down into his lungs.

He opened his eyes with a supreme effort, took another look around. It was almost full dark by now but he could just make out the shapes of the other birds around him; every one of them lay full length, not one moved. One buzzard had fallen in the hedge, the other lay on top of it, spread-eagled on the spikey hawthorn branches, its head hanging down.

Fal took another step, his legs and his balance deserted him. He fell forward, lay with his head supported by a springy tussock of grass. He could not even manage to move his position so he gave up trying. It was comfortable enough, pillowed in readiness for a long, deep sleep.

He felt himself drifting, a feeling akin to letting a current of air take him when he was in full flight; so relaxing. He would sleep like the others, and when morning came they would all be refreshed. He would take Li back to the Soldiers' Wood and they would make their home there. For ever.

Chapter Twelve

Shaf, the leader of the badger colony which lived in the small island of age-old deciduous trees in the midst of the vast conifer plantations, was puzzled. Not uneasy, not yet, anyway, because the changes that had taken place did not affect the badgers.

Shaf was lying in the entrance to the big sett one afternoon, basking in the gentle warmth of the autumn sunshine, when he saw the two strange birds arrive. His eyesight was poor yet he was acutely aware of everything that went on in and around this small wood that was hidden away from Man.

Shaf was familiar with buzzards, their slow wingbeats and feline calling; sometimes they came here to sit motionless for hours on a branch of one of the majestic oaks, waiting for a rabbit to hop within reach. And Spi, the sparrowhawk, who had lived here as long as the badgers could remember, and who flew fast and silently, took woodpigeons in full flight. And there were the kestrels that hovered with rapid wingbeats and whose eyesight was keen enough to spot a mouse on the leafy floor.

Shaf knew all of these but the hawks that arrived and made their home up in the lofty branches were a mystery to him. At first he thought that they might be large sparrowhawks, maybe cousins of Spi, but their calling was different, a high-pitched *ca-ca* or *gek-gek*, nothing like the long drawn-out *pee-eew* of the sparrowhawk.

Shaf was curious; rarely did he come across anything unfamiliar in his small world. Mostly the badgers foraged for food after dark and the only birds of prey which they encountered were owls, noisy birds that sometimes screeched throughout the whole of a moonlight night. These newcomers went up to roost at dusk and did not show themselves again until break of day. They were a kind of sparrowhawk but not quite a sparrowhawk. He left it at that, but he would certainly keep a lookout for them.

Badger Wood was no longer just the domain of the badgers, there were other species, both furred and feathered, who sought sanctuary here from humans. Raol, the carrion crow and his mate, Cau, had taken up residence last Spring. Constantly persecuted by Reuben, Raol recognized the wood as being almost inaccessible to the gamekeeper; it was a long hard trek through the dense conifers which isolated it from the surrounding landscape. And yet, for those who could fly, it was only a short distance from the game preserves. Raol and Cau hunted far and wide, their depredations were widespread, there were few nests between here and the village that were well enough hidden to escape them. Their cunning was second to none which was why they had survived. They enjoyed the best of the human world as well as their own.

For much the same reason Spi had moved to Badger Wood. His mate, Sa, had been shot by the gamekeeper; Spi had been on his own for two seasons now. There were few sparrowhawks in Hopwas Wood, those that had not been killed had sought safety elsewhere. Spi occasionally glimpsed another of his own kind in passing. Badger Wood was the safest place of all; he always returned here, seldom went too far away from it. Perhaps, one day, a female sparrowhawk would seek refuge here. So far one hadn't.

Badger Wood was the only place now where there were

rabbits to be found. Their survival was due to their isolation from other warrens, for the terrible disease that had wiped them out in other places was carried by fleas and passed from one rabbit to another in close confinement. And as these rabbits never met up with any others of their own kind, they were spared. Which was fortunate for the natural predators around Badger Wood.

Foxes prowled here occasionally but they were not welcomed by the badgers except during a temporary emergency such as pursuit by the Hunt. Shaf had noticed last Winter, though, that the few foxes that travelled this far did not catch many rabbits. In fact, they seemed incompetent where hunting was concerned. That was fine by him for he did not want the rabbits exterminated. The badgers only took young rabbits, their main diet was earthworms and there was an inexhaustible supply of those beneath the thick carpet of dead leaves that covered the floor of the wood.

Spi killed a rabbit occasionally, usually he concentrated his efforts on the pigeons that used the adjacent conifers as a roost. The rabbits had bred well this Summer, Shaf could not remember seeing so many before. Of course, the increase in population lured Sacko, the stoat, here; and Were, the weasel, and his mate, Oboz. They were really bloodthirsty hunters; by night rabbits unfortunate enough to be caught by these small fierce animals squealed their terror. Shaf hoped that the two species between them would not wipe out the rabbits. Thankfully, Pyne, the polecat, had moved on elsewhere, and hadn't been seen for a long, long time now. He had been the worst of the rabbit slayers.

But now something was killing the rabbits with alarming regularity.

The badgers held a council over the rabbit deaths. It wasn't foxes, they usually carried their kill away with them. If they caught any! Stoats and weasels left a distinctive mark on the back of their victims' necks and only occasionally was a dead rabbit identified as their handiwork; Pyne was no longer here to kill. Spi was entitled to his quota, the badgers had come across the remains of his lightning strikes. In fact, the kills which they found bore a remarkable similarity to those of the sparrowhawk but surely even Spi was not able to strip the unfortunate creatures of virtually every vestige of flesh!

What, then, was killing the rabbits with such alarming regularity that the badgers already saw their numbers declining? Shaf discovered the answer to this on another warm autumn day as he alternately dozed and kept watch at the entrance to the sett.

It was the strange hawks that were slaughtering the rabbits!

Although Shaf's hearing was far superior to his eyesight, he heard nothing. Some strange instinct, an inbuilt alarm system that seldom failed to warn of pending danger, caused his sleepy eyes to flicker open. A rabbit was grazing the grass in the clearing; one moment it was eating contentedly, the next a shadow fell across it and the smaller of the two hawks struck with unerring accuracy and a speed that was too fast for a badger's eye to follow.

Almost immediately the larger hawk alighted beside his mate; together they began to strip the rabbit of its fur. Only when their hunger was satisfied did they leave, fly away as silently as they had come.

It was all very worrying. Shaf called another council of the badgers but there appeared to be no solution to the problem. Certainly, they could survive without rabbits; foxes, stoats and weasels could hunt elsewhere and Spi would doubtless find his rabbits further afield. But young rabbits were a delicacy to be enjoyed in Spring and Summer so why should the badgers be deprived of them by two strange massive sparrowhawks? It wasn't as if they could discuss the matter with the hawks; Spi was beyond their means of communication. Sacko, Were and Oboz could be warned off, threatened. But there was nothing that they could do about the hawks.

Each evening since the Spring a blackbird had warbled its evensong from the top of a hawthorn bush that grew over the sett. Not that the badgers found it particularly musical, it merely heralded the approaching dusk. They stirred in the galleries where they had slept throughout the day, knew that it was almost time to go up above and forage for food.

One evening the bird didn't sing. The badgers noticed its absence but often wild creatures changed their habits. Perhaps it had found a place more to its liking. Then they discovered a pile of feathers on the ground beneath the thorn bush; more feathers adhered to the prickly branches. The bird had been struck down even before it uttered its first note, a predator had watched its dusk routine and swooped down upon it from the tall trees that surrounded the clearing.

Now the hawks had begun to decimate the small bird population of Badger Wood.

Badger Wood was much to the goshawks' liking. In fact, it was the best habitat they had discovered since their release into the wild. There had been rabbits in plenty; these were fewer now and much more wary, often choosing to graze by night. Garn and Ka had hunted the small bird population ruthlessly, even these were becoming scarcer in and around the wood.

And then, as the leaves turned a deep golden and began to fall, flocks of fieldfares arrived, weary after their long flight from Russia and eastern Europe. The goshawks were familiar with fieldfares, and their call of *chack-chack* as these thrush-like birds flighted jerkily back from the fields each evening.

There were certainly enough fieldfares to satisfy two hungry hawks who had once again exhausted their readily available supply of food.

But all the birds who came to Badger Wood were not welcomed by the goshawks. One day as they flew around the outskirts in search of a pigeon that might have returned to the trees for a day roost whilst it digested a crop full of acorns, some crows suddenly appeared.

Garn recognized the belligerent caw-caw, the high-pitched note becoming a growl that was taken up by the other half-dozen crows. The corvids were perching in a sycamore that had lost its leaves, black silhouettes against a blustery sky. Wings opened, flapped, and the birds began cavorting above the hawks.

The goshawks could easily have outdistanced their tormentors but, as so often happens, they did not even attempt to flee. They swerved, dived, perhaps once the aerial contest began they enjoyed it as much as the crows.

Flying to and fro, engaging in aerobatics, it was all a kind of game today. What had brought the crows here, for they were seldom seen beyond their conifer woods, was something that did not even occur to the beleagured goshawks.

The corn was all harvested, the fields ploughed; crows and terns are usually only attracted to freshly turned soil. Perhaps the wireworms had burrowed deep since then, and the fields no longer attracted predators. There was no carrion on the grassland; food was scarce for crows, too, and they were lured to Badger Wood, if only to perch in the tall trees for conifers are rarely conducive to them.

Whatever the reason, they were here and their incessant loud calling attracted others of their kind from afar. Wavy lines of rooks and jackdaws battled against the stiff breeze as they came from every direction.

Soon the hills were a cacophony of raucousness, a clamour of vindictive mischief. Garn and Ka weaved, swerved, outdistanced their aggressors for short periods and then, for some inexplicable reason, returned to the fray. Beaks snapped but none made contact.

Eventually, both crows and goshawks tired of this pointless game; Garn and Ka retired to the wood, the crows drifted away in bunches. Tomorrow they might return to do further battle.

The affray had not gone unnoticed. Below the hills and on the outskirts of the village, Reuben had watched the distant milling specks with more than just casual interest. There was a gleam in his eyes which had not been there since that day when Vinny had ruined their chances of exterminating the goshawks in Hopwas Wood.

Chapter Thirteen

*T*he pheasants had long left the questionable safety of the release pen, were fending for themselves in the wilds of Hopwas Wood. The foxes didn't kill many of them, their cunning was not what it used to be; a stalk often resulted in the birds fluttering up to safety in the trees because they had heard their enemy approaching downwind. Foxes always, without fail, used to stalk their intended prey upwind and even then moved silently. Not nowadays, it seemed. The pheasants perched on branches out of the reach of the fox that jumped up in a futile attempt to dislodge them; they became braver as the weeks passed and they matured, mocked their enemy.

Reuben and Vinny spent their days carrying corn to the feeding points and patrolling with their guns. They shot more foxes than ever before because the animals were slow to react, easily lured with a decoy call, and some even appeared to be fearless of humans.

One afternoon Vinny saw Reuben approaching him with a haste that was in itself disturbing. When Reuben hurried, something was amiss and blame was not long in falling upon his chosen scapegoat.

"I know where those gosses are!" The gamekeeper was clearly excited.

"They're gone," Vinny answered. "Never seen 'em since that day when . . ."

"Because they've been hidin' out in Badger Wood!" Reuben thumped a fist into the palm of his hand. "Never thought of lookin' for 'em *there*! I ought to've guessed, the habitat's right and the rabbits up there have probably escaped the myxy. The crows have been mobbin' 'em all morning, they wouldn't bother that long with sparrowhawks. And what a grand place to do 'em in, right away from anybody who might be spyin' on us. Even Swift and Jackson don't get up to Badger Wood."

"It'd take you half a day to force your way through the conifer wood and, even if you made it, the gosses would hear you coming and they'd be long gone by the time you got there." Vinny was disturbed at the prospect of being despatched to that small wood on the steep hillside. "Remember how those two SAS recruits got lost in there on that exercise in the Summer? Recruitin' for an elite unit, they were, and in the end they had to holler for help and give themselves up to the Hunter Force!"

"They were raw recruits, that's why. There's a way up, all right. You follow the stream, it's hard going and very steep, but eventually it'll bring you right out by the hardwood trees."

"Oh!" Vinny swallowed. He did not relish the idea of crawling up that watercourse, the water would be icy, the rocks slippery with moss and lichen. It wasn't a nice place at all. "Like I said, you'd make so much noise that the goshawks would hear you comin'."

"They might hear you, but not *me*!" There was undisguised contempt in Reuben's sneer. "You'll do all the work here tomorrow whilst *I* go."

"Oh, sure!" Vinny's relief was only too apparent. Work was not his favourite occupation but far rather the most laborious jobs that Reuben could think up than a trip up there. "That's fine, I'll top up all the feeding points, and I'll do the rounds of the snares and traps and . . ."

"You do that," Reuben's expression became furtive, "and if anybody asks where I've gone, I've gone up to Badger Wood after a fox that's been troublin' us for weeks. Got it? Just in case anybody hears me shootin' . . ."

Reuben prepared himself for his arduous trek. He donned camouflage clothing that blended with the background of fir trees, and wellington boots because the stream would be deep in places. He took the shotgun in preference to the rifle, a blast of shot was more accurate than a single bullet in such surroundings. Noise was of no consequence, he had already left his alibi with his assistant.

He set off soon after daylight and took a short cut through Hopwas Wood that brought him out on to the fields bordering the conifer plantation.

The crows' angry chorus had already begun in the distance; he focused his binoculars, made out a flock of black birds soaring, swooping. Mobbing.

The goshawks were up there, all right.

He followed the stream alongside the fir wood; the water was low after the dry summer, it gurgled over stones, in places there were small still pools where minnows darted.

Suddenly the watercourse turned abruptly into the conifers. This was where the going became difficult. Low branches obstructed his progress, some he crawled beneath, others he pushed to one side. One sprang back, slapped him across the face; the pointed leaves were sharp and drew a trickle of blood. It was as if Nature was protecting her own.

He slipped, banged his knee and was forced to rest awhile. Maybe he should have gone in from the Black Hill side, the trees were just as dense but it was a downward climb all the way to Badger Wood. With hindsight the alternative would have been preferable but it was too late now. He had come too far to turn back.

He paused to listen; all around was so still in this dark and gloomy place. He could not hear the crows any longer but that was because thickly planted woods muffled sound. He could not even hear the traffic on the distant main road.

From now on the terrain rose steeply, in places the stream was a veritable waterfall. He grasped large rocks to pull himself up; everywhere was slippery, a cold dank world where the sunlight never penetrated.

The grey feathers which adhered to a tree stood out starkly in the half light, bizarre Christmas tree decorations, tinsel that had tarnished and drooped. He had been expecting to come upon some so he would have been disappointed if he had not. If the goshawks were here then they had to hunt to survive.

His experienced eye saw at a glance what had happened. A woodpigeon had settled at the top of the spruce tree to digest its food and a goshawk had surprised it. A swift kill, only the feathers were left to tell the tale. Reuben nodded his satisfaction, the feathers were still dry so the goshawk had killed only a short time ago – yesterday afternoon there had been a heavy shower of rain. The trail was getting warm.

The heavy silence was broken by the screeching of a jay. It called twice from close by; the next shriek was deep in the plantation. It had seen him and was spreading the alarm. Seldom did humans infiltrate Nature's remotest domain without being spotted. He waited for a few minutes. The bird did not call again.

There was a clatter of wings as some pigeons took off; they had been day-roosting and he had crept within twenty yards of them. Their presence was a sure sign that the hawks weren't in the immediate vicinity. He hadn't expected his quest to be that easy. Patience and stealth were the key to success; when he found the goshawks he would only get one chance.

He had some difficulty surmounting a huge boulder that

blocked his path. The stream divided, trickled by on either side. He knew that he was almost at the source of the water-course and beyond it lay Badger Wood.

He managed to clamber over the moss-covered rock, saw daylight beyond the firs. Bent double, he crept forward, gun at the ready. Crouched, he stared at the scene which greeted him.

The small wood was truly majestic, the aroma that met him was one of bygone days, the sweet-sour smell of decaying vegetation, of a world where nothing had changed for a century or more.

Regal trees that had defied Winter after Winter, twisted boughs that had refused to yield to the elements. A mass of briars rose up like a final bastion to deter any who might have braved the rigours so far. Their juicy fruit was tempting, it might have been poisoned by some wicked witch to protect her home from intruders.

Reuben was not a fanciful person, he scoffed at all but stark reality. This place was a wilderness; the trees would have been felled, the earth ploughed and planted with sap-lings like the surrounding landscape but for the fact that it was an oasis of deep slate that was impossible to cultivate. The ancient trees had found a roothold, they had been reprieved. The foresters had spared the wood and it had become a haven for predators beyond his own jurisdiction. But not today.

His practised eye saw a narrow track running through the briars; made by badgers, undoubtedly, and the brambles were less dense here. The run led to the interior of the small wood.

Reuben hesitated, he was suddenly aware that the crows were not calling any longer. He scanned the sky through the high branches – there was not a bird of any species in sight. Which meant that the goshawks had left the wood and there was no reason for the corvids to remain here.

But he had half expected that to be the case for rarely do

birds of prey remain in a small area throughout the day. They fly off to scour the surrounding landscape.

He followed the track through the brambles which brought him to a wide clearing with mounds of earth long overgrown with vegetation; he saw a wide hole with a well-used track leading from it. He explored the undergrowth, found more tracks and holes. There were badgers living here, this was the largest sett he had ever come across, and that was worth bearing in mind!

Stealthily, he crept between the mighty boles; he came upon evidence of several more goshawk kills; some pigeon feathers, a rabbit's fur and bones, and there were fieldfare feathers stuck to the brambles. For a time these few acres of traditional woodland had been a paradise for the hawks, they had reaped a full harvest and were now hunting further afield.

Some stains on the ground attracted his attention; he knelt to examine them. A lifetime's experience learning to identify the droppings of every animal and bird that inhabited the woodlands told him that these had come from goshawks. Their concentration in one place meant that this was a roost tree. His gaze travelled up the towering beech, its trunk was splashed white all the way down.

Reuben nodded his satisfaction to himself. He had found what he was looking for. Towards dusk the goshawks would return. And he would be waiting for them.

Chapter Fourteen

Garn and Ka found themselves on unfamiliar territory. It had not been their intention to go on up to the moors that lay far beyond Hopwas Wood but the crows had driven them there with their incessant harrassment. This time sheer speed had left their tormentors far behind; the corvids had followed them for some distance and then tired of the pursuit. There were still a few wireworms to be found on the ploughed land and there was always the possibility of coming upon some carrion on the pastureland. The flock split up, went their separate ways.

Up on the moorland rolling heather stretched as far as the eye could see, interspersed with patches of scrubland, mostly silver birch thickets. Rowan trees grew here and there, their berries bright red. A buzzard soared, floated in the wind.

The neat whitewashed shepherd's cottage stood by the side of the rough track that wound down from the road. Some large birds were feeding on the area of grass at the rear, similar in size to pheasants but darker in colour. A cock bird was perched on the post and rail fence; he saw the goshawks approaching from afar and uttered a piercing call of *kok . . . kok . . . kok . . . gobak-gobak*. They were guinea fowl.

The other birds reacted instantly, flew up into the clump

of thick firs which had been planted as a wind-break for the dwelling. Only when the dense foliage had swallowed them up did the big black bird follow; his role was that of protector, the safety of his hens was paramount if the species was to survive up here. Hawks were their natural enemies; sparrowhawks only troubled them during the summer months when the hens were rearing their young but occasionally a red kite and a peregrine falcon appeared on the moors. He did not know what these newcomers were but their very size and speed was menacing.

Manquhill and Cornharrow were places of sheer magnificence, large tracts of land that had not yet been spoiled by the unsightly symmetry of economic forestry. Sheep grazed in places but not in sufficient numbers to decimate the fresh growth of heather so important to the survival of the grouse and blackgame.

In the early months of every year the old shepherd burned the area of old heather, taking great care that the fire was controlled. This promoted the new growth; it was an age-old ritual; when he retired it was doubtful whether a younger replacement would continue with the moor-burning. If not, the grouse would be deprived of their natural diet and their population would decrease; they might even die out altogether. But, for the moment, old-fashioned conservation continued here.

Amidst the fading purple of the heather a reddish-brown colouring attracted Garn's searching gaze. With Ka close behind, he approached it warily, flew in decreasing circles until he was close enough to identify it. It was a fox and Garn knew by the way it lay full length that it was dead. Its head lolled to one side, it was so thin that in places its bones almost protruded through its mangy skin.

It lay in a small hollow close to a brackish, peaty pool. It had struggled here in search of water but it had not managed the last few yards. Garn knew it had not been chased by the

Hunt; there were no ugly wounds, no visible means of violent death. It had simply starved.

The goshawks were puzzled. Dead creatures were almost never seen in the wild. Then the rabbits had begun dying out in the open, carrion for scavenging species. Now it seemed that the foxes were suffering a similar fate.

Garn and Ka flew on, only if they were ravenous and there was no other food to be had would they have eaten the rancid flesh of a carnivore.

They experienced a new sense of freedom. Manquhill was so wild, the sheep were the only evidence that humans had infiltrated here. There was just one fence, a straggling line of rotting posts and rusted barbed wire that hung loosely; in places it had fallen and wool fluttered on the barbs where the sheep had meandered through. The birds were not to know that this was an almost forgotten boundary between the two moors. Over the years they had merged, for the ownership of land in this remoteness was not of great importance. The neighbouring shepherds knew which were their sheep, they would not round up those which were not theirs when Winter approached and it was necessary to bring the animals down from high ground.

A covey of red grouse sprang with a suddenness that surprised even the goshawks; the birds were nervous and as alert as the sentinel of their larger cousins up by the cottage. They burst up from the heather, hurtled down the long slope, their whirring wings giving them incredible speed. Garn and Ka arrowed in pursuit, barely skimming the bushy growth.

The covey was a dozen strong, kept close together; gliding, accelerating, gliding again. Garn knew that he and his mate were catching up on them, gained height in readiness for a swift, downward strike. And then, just as suddenly as they had sprung, the grouse set their wings and alighted in a dense patch of heather. And were gone.

The goshawks glided on. Perhaps there were more grouse here and the next time they would have better luck. They were hungry, they had not eaten since leaving Badger Wood. They quartered; in their own instinctive methodical way they covered almost every clump of heather as they worked their way up on to the even higher ground of Cornharrow.

Here there were patches of scree, shale slopes and rocky outcrops. The heather was more sparse, a grey and barren landscape that was the habitat for no creature because there was nothing to eat and no shelter, just a leaden, lowering sky beyond the horizon. An environment where nothing lived.

Or so it seemed to the goshawks. Until a movement, a trickle of loose shale attracted their attention. There was a miniature avalanche, stones rattling, a shape camouflaged against its background so that it was barely noticeable. An animal; it bounded, ran, slithered as it struggled to keep a foothold on the scree.

A rabbit!

This time Ka was the first to swoop; wings arrowed, she thrust ahead of Garn, struck the scrabbling rabbit unerringly. She lifted it, carried it as far as a platform of flat rock.

Even as Garn made to follow her, another rabbit started up from close by, its panic-stricken flight hampered by the steep and treacherous slope. Its only hope of survival would have been to bolt downhill, squeeze into one of several niches in the rock face below that had often saved it from the claws of peregrine falcons. A rabbit's instinct, though, is to run uphill. Garn had it before it had covered a couple of metres; soon he was feasting alongside Ka on that rocky shelf worn smooth by the elements over the centuries.

The goshawks remained there for some time after they had finished eating. The sheer wildness of this place enthralled them, there wasn't a human habitation in sight. They were reluctant to return to their former home.

Some time later they flew again. This time, though, they were not hunting for they were well satisfied; they were savouring the freshness of a moorland westerly, the rich aroma of heather. They scented the sweet smell of pines and glided where it led them.

The firs grew in a hollow beyond the next horizon, planted as a shelter for moorland sheep on either side of a fast flowing stream, mature trees that offered shelter for both birds and beasts. The goshawks alighted on a top branch, surveyed their new kingdom until the first stars twinkled in a dusky sky. Only then did they shuffle along to the trunk. It was snug and warm beneath the thick branches. Tomorrow was another day.

They hunted soon after first light. There were numerous rabbits on and around the scree, rock dwellers who grazed the scrubland, gnawed the bark of birch and rowan trees when the tough grass became unpalatable during the Winter.

These rabbits were fleet of foot and far more alert to danger than their counterparts in lowland areas. Here there was a constant threat from hawks and foxes. On their journeys to and from their slate warrens to their grazing, they were vulnerable; on successive mornings Garn and Ka intercepted their prey on the slippery scree. After that the rabbits were wiser and more cunning: they braved the pre-dawn darkness to travel, hid in shallow bolt holes in the scrub thickets by day. For a time the goshawks had to content themselves with fieldfares that came here in numbers after the glut of rowan berries.

Soon they became adept at hunting grouse; they learned that chasing coveys was mostly futile, the birds flew until their wings were tired and then alighted and hid in the dense heather. Sometimes it was difficult to put them up at all because at the first sign of a hawk of any species the grouse crouched motionless in cover, remained there until the danger was past.

Garn and Ka took it in turn to sit motionless in a scrub wood whilst the other quartered the heather slopes. Their prey would either flush or sit tight, depending on weather conditions. On still days they often flew, that familiar down-hill glide aided by whirring wings. They were no match for an intercepting goshawk; they were convinced that the danger lay behind them. Sometimes the goshawks put up the same covey two or three times, the grouse were nervous and panicked after one kill.

When the snow came the grouse were easy prey; they no longer blended with their surroundings, those familiar dark blobs could be spotted from on high. They were often to be found scratching on the snow-packed rough road, for grit is vital to a grouse's diet. One by one, the big grouse covey was depleted to single numbers long before the breeding season arrived.

The rabbits were culled drastically. They, too, were vulnerable in severe weather. But a swift death is preferable to a lingering one from disease. Excessive numbers, even up here on the moors, would have brought disease in some form. Or starvation.

Garn and Ka had no desire to return to Black Hill or Hopwas Wood; by now they had forgotten their homeland. It was as though they had known nowhere except this expanse of moor, that they had never roosted anywhere else but in the fir wood alongside the rushing brook.

Chapter Fifteen

Walter drove out to the countryside from the city most weeks during the winter months. Tall and imposing with a neatly trimmed beard, he wore lovat green clothing and a matching Tryolean hat. He was respected by farmers and shepherds alike for his role in life was that of a falconer.

His fame was nationwide, he was booked at most of the major country shows to put on a display of falconry which enthralled the watching crowds. He also bred and trained falcons in a mode of hunting that went back to Roman times. During the course of training these birds, he culled rabbits and pigeons which destroyed crops. Far rather, landowners decided, that Walter went quietly and methodically about this business than men with guns banged away, disturbing the peace and quiet and frightening livestock.

Walter trained and worked several species of hawks but goshawks wore his favourite; they were majestic in appearance, a delight to watch in full flight.

Today was special for Walter. Perched on his padded arm as he walked up the steep slope towards Black Hill was a beautiful hen goshawk who had only this season reached maturity; so intelligent, so gentle, the short leather leg strap with a swivel and leash were a precaution rather than a necessity. Walter never took chances, some strange noise might frighten her and send her flying in panic to the forest. A small bell was attached to one of her legs just in case she did happen to get lost on her first full flight.

He talked soothingly to her, she had all the makings of a fine hunter. Today was her ultimate test; he had every confidence in her.

All the rabbits were gone now, so Farmer Davies's son had told him, myxomatosis had virtually exterminated them in these hills. Occasionally Walter brought a ferret with him to flush rabbits from their burrows for the falcons to chase; today he had left the ferret in its hutch at home. Woodpigeons would be Tass's quarry this afternoon, he had noticed a few flying over the forest. He decided to climb to the very top of the hill, work his way back down; the first pigeon that broke cover would be Tass's big test.

He had heard that somebody had been laying poisoned bait in the sheep fields. A number of dead buzzards and crows had been found and the forestry rangers were concerned because some young goshawks had not been seen lately. There were whispered rumours that the culprit was Hughes, the old farmer; others blamed Reuben, the gamekeeper. But there was no proof to substantiate these accusations.

Walter was slightly uneasy about flying Tass but she wouldn't drop down to carrion, not whilst there was live prey to be had, he was certain of that. All the same, it was a worrying thought.

It took him nearly an hour to reach the summit of the hill. Beyond the far horizon lay the two moors, Cornharrow and Manquhill. Walter dared not risk going any further because there were grouse in the heather and the owners would be displeased if their birds were scattered by a hunting hawk. On his right was the Black Hill, and on his left , lower down, stretched acres and acres of commercial spruce. In the midst of these, towering above the symmetrically planted trees, was a strange little wood of oak and beech, their golden leaves in stark contrast to the deep green all around.

That wood had always intrigued Walter, it was so mysterious. He had often thought about going there. Maybe one day he would, just to see what it was like. It would be like stepping back a hundred years in time, walking through woodland that was how this landscape once was before greed dominated and all that people thought about was making money out of the environment. Maybe one day he would make an effort to visit the place, force his way through the closely growing firs. At least from here it was downhill all the way; the return journey would be the most difficult.

A pigeon flapped lazily out of the nearest conifers; it had not seen Walter, the bright sunlight was in its eyes if it looked in an uphill direction. It had fed all morning, returned to the forest to digest the contents of its bulging crop and now it was going back to the fields to feed again.

"Go, girl!" Walter slipped the leash on Tass's leg; she needed no second bidding, she had seen the grey bird, knew what was expected of her.

She sped away, flew straight and true, instinctively low at first so that the trees would hide her from her prey until she gained upon it. Walter marvelled at her speed and grace, already she showed traits of a superb hunting hawk.

But the woodpigeon did not flap and glide downhill as he had expected; probably it was taking advantage of a cross current of the stiff breeze and it headed back across the firs. Perhaps its feeding grounds were on the other side by Hopwas Wood or the Soldiers' Wood. It was certainly gaining speed now, a distant grey speck. When Tass rose above the firs she might not see it; maybe another pigeon would clatter out of the trees and she would strike away in pursuit of that. Which was the last thing Walter wanted; he prided himself that his trained birds chased the prey he had directed them to.

If the pigeon had continued on a downhill course it would

have been an ideal chase for Tass. But it had changed direction.

Walter gasped aloud his admiration for Tass. She soared above the conifers, her hesitation was only momentary. She had seen the distant pigeon and now she was hurtling after it. It looked like being a long chase, far longer than he had intended for a first attempt, but now it was beyond his control.

Walter had expected the pigeon to increase its speed now that it had determined where it was going. Instead it gained height, clapped its wings, slowed, went into a glide. What on earth was happening? Had it merely fancied a change of day roost? Certainly it was about to settle.

Suddenly, Walter understood. The woodpigeon was dropping down into Badger Wood because the acorns and beechmast offered a tempting meal! And Tass was not far behind it. She would catch it for sure.

Walter thrilled to the chase, watched in fascination. There, the pigeon gave one final flap of its wings, glided down. He could not see it any longer, it was doubtless perched on a branch, surveying the scattering of food on the ground. Then it would drop down to feed. Most likely Tass would take it before it got that far.

Walter could barely make out the goshawk, a streak above the treetops. Some more pigeons lifted further down, scattered in alarm. But her course was straight and true, she did not change direction and go for them. Tass had exceeded even the experienced falconer's expectations. This was a bird he would talk of for many years to come.

The pigeons were out of sight and he had one final glimpse of Tass arrowing in on those giant trees. Now he could see her no longer. Was that a puff of feathers? More than likely he was seeing what he wanted to see, envisaging the swift kill.

There was no movement to be seen, neither crows nor pigeons. Nothing. Doubtless Tass had killed and would be feathering her prey. She would stop to feed briefly. And then, if she remembered her training, she would fly straight back to her master. Walter stood and waited.

A few minutes later a muffled bang erupted from somewhere on the wooded hillside. Walter started, heard the echoes gather and roll. Sounds were difficult to pinpoint up in these hills; you thought they came from a certain direction but the contours fooled you. That report might have been as far away as Hopwas Wood, even Soldiers' Wood. It could have been a bird-scarer in one of the fields, set to deter marauding crows or pigeons from a growing crop. If so it would go off again in a minute or two.

Or quarry blasting. A detonation that would not be repeated. Somewhere a cock pheasant voiced its protest at the disturbance, then all went quiet again.

It might even have been a gunshot. Realistically, Walter decided, that was the most probable solution. A syndicate from the city rented the shooting over most of these woods and on winter weekends the hills echoed to the sound of gunfire. But today was a weekday, there had only been a single report. The gamekeepers were always patrolling their preserves, if they came upon a fox or a crow, they shot it. That was what had happened, he was convinced.

Tass would be back in a few minutes. Well, he'd give her a quarter of an hour, it was her first kill and she would doubtless linger over the experience. It was always nerve-racking with a trainee, one worried about their return. Excited by their success, they might fly off in search of another victim. Not Tass, though, he had an uncanny confidence in her, she was a 'natural'. She would come flying back shortly, circle above him and drop straight down on to his extended arm. Of course, she would.

He stood and waited.

Chapter Sixteen

Walter was becoming increasingly concerned. He checked his watch and scanned the fir thickets alternately. Tass should have returned by now. Doubtless she had stayed to feed on her prey, that was only natural after a first kill. The distance from where he stood down to that clump of hardwoods amidst the conifers was negligible in terms of goshawk travel. Even flying leisurely after gorging herself, she would have been back with him in a minute or two.

He never even considered that some mishap had befallen her. He thought one of two things had happened; she had become excited by her success and had gone in search of another woodpigeon or she could have flown in any direction. Consequently, she had become lost, or most certainly would be by the time she had tired of hunting. She might even have killed again but she would not linger to feed a second time. Or else she was perched in one of those distant tall trees digesting her meal. The longer the delay, the less she would remember where to return.

He was too far away to hear the tinkling of the bell attached to her leg. He was faced with a dilemma; either he waited here in the hope that she would find him or he went to look for her. He had to choose between the lesser of two evils; whilst he was forcing his way through the dense plantation she might return and she certainly would not see him in there, but the longer she was away, the less likely she was to remember where he was.

His instinct was to go and try to find her. He walked slowly towards the fringe of the conifers, paused for one last look around. There wasn't a bird to be seen in the sky. He began to force his way through the trees, stooping between the evenly planted rows, crawling in places where the prickly branches grew low and impassable.

After a hundred yards or so he doubted the wisdom of his decision.

Reuben recognized the woodpigeon's wingbeats as it came from behind where he crouched. He knew from experience what it was going to do, wings extended to slow its speed. In other woods it might have circled, made a reconnaissance to ensure that all was safe. But in Badger Wood there was never any danger, no lurking hunter. Except now – but the pigeon didn't know that, it had no reason for suspicion.

It alighted on a branch to the gamekeeper's left; he watched it with lowered head from his ambush point; it sat relaxed. Doubtless it had come here after the acorns and beechmast. Shortly it would drop down to the ground and begin scratching in the dead leaves. Reuben made no attempt to raise his gun, he had not come here after pigeons.

One moment the bird was sitting contemplating its food, the next it was knocked from its perch in a cloud of feathers. This time there was no rush of wings, the attacker arrived with the silence and speed of an archer's arrow. A bell tinkled on impact but at the time its significance was lost on the human observer.

Feathers floated in the air with the serenity of a flurry of snowflakes. The pigeon thudded softly on to a thick mass of leaves. Almost instantly its attacker was upon it, clawing at its victim's breast to bare the flesh, gouging it with its beak. The bell jangled but Reuben was too preoccupied to notice it.

Very slowly he brought the butt of the shotgun up to his shoulder, his hands trembled so that the twin barrels quivered. He had not expected the goshawks to return yet, he had conditioned himself for a lengthy vigil until dusk. They must have been hunting close by, had seen the pigeon come in to land and followed it.

Where was the second hawk? It was unlikely to be far away from its mate. Reuben glanced both ways out of the corner of his eye but there was no sign of the other goshawk. He had hoped that they might arrive together and give him the opportunity to kill the pair. He had two cartridges in his gun and never once doubted his own ability as a marksman.

The goshawk was ravenously mutilating its prey; Reuben was faced with a decision. He could either blast it as it fed or wait in the hope that the other arrived to join its mate.

A bird in the hand is worth two in the bush; it was an old but very true saying. Reuben's fingers rested on the trigger. The sound of the shot would almost certainly frighten the other goshawk away but if he delayed and the bird happened to spot him, he might lose both of them. He knew what he had to do.

The gun barrels wavered in his grip, he waited for them to steady. He took a deep breath and held it. The goshawk was engrossed in its meal and did not look up. Reuben squeezed the trigger; the blast was deafening in that small wood nestling amidst the firs; the gun barrels jerked upwards but not before their charge of shot had sped true and devastatingly.

The gamekeeper let out his pent up breath, stared at the pile of limp feathers. It had been a point blank shot but that was immaterial, it wasn't a pheasant intended for the pot.

There was a roaring in his ears, the gunshot had been magnified within this enclosed wood. Now he heard it rolling away, it seemed to echo in all directions. Nobody would be able to pinpoint whence it had come, and, even if they did, Vinny had Reuben's alibi prepared. A fox had met its end, one of those from the city, dumped by well-meaning but misguided do-gooders. Reuben had mercifully put it out of its suffering, otherwise it would have starved to a lingering death.

He straightened up, moved out of his hiding place. All sorts of doubts began to nag him; at a glance the bird had seemed smaller than those that had occupied the larch on Black Hill in the Summer. It wasn't a sparrowhawk by any chance, was it? He grabbed for an outstretched broken wing, lifted the bird aloft by it. He saw the bell hanging from its leg as it tinkled, stared aghast.

This was a falcon, a hawk bred in captivity for the sport of hunting!

Reuben was both dismayed and angry. This wasn't one of the goshawks he had come up here for; he realized only too well where it had come from. It belonged to that falconer fellow, the chap the forestry allowed to go hawking in the hills. Reuben had once protested to Swift about it but the ranger had not relented, had claimed that Walter only hunted rabbits and pigeons and that the trained hawks would not harm pheasants. Poppycock! But that did not alter the fact that Reuben had shot a falcon and that its owner was probably not far away.

The gamekeeper deliberated what to do. Doubtless the falconer would have heard the shot, he *might* have pinpointed it as coming from here. In which case he might be waiting for Reuben at the point where the stream entered the wood, the fellow was familiar with his surroundings.

First, Reuben had to get rid of the incriminating evidence. He did not have a spade with which to bury the dead goshawk and, even if he had, the ground here was virtually solid slate and digging would have been an impossibility. He could shove it down a rabbit hole, heel the loose soil in to close the entrance. Except that the rabbits here had their warrens deep in the briars . . .

There would be nowhere to bury it in the surrounding conifer wood, the trees were planted close together, even with a spade he would not be able to make a hole deep enough. If he left the goshawk here, it might well be found and the finger of suspicion would point unerringly at himself.

He had an idea, a cunning one. The falconer would be expecting him to emerge at the bottom, the stream was the only way down. But, if he headed out towards the Black Hill, that would foil any attempt to catch him. And Hughes's field was within walking distance, that was where the big rabbit warren was situated. Reuben could stuff the hawk down a rabbit hole there and if it was discovered then suspicion would revert to the farmer. There were whispers in the village that Hughes had been laying poison for crows and hawks so nobody would be surprised that he'd shot one and tried to hide it.

Reuben grinned to himself, began the irksome task of negotiating the conifer thicket in a north-westerly direction. It was uphill all the way but the trees would have slowed his progress whatever the gradient. He ripped the bell off the dangling leg to stop it jangling; his clothes were smeared with blood. Fox's blood!

That pair of goshawks had eluded him but their day would come, he promised himself that. At least this tame hawk wouldn't be hunting the game preserves any longer so some good had come out of this episode.

It was impossible to move quietly; branches swished and slapped loudly against his clothing, his booted feet cracked dead twigs. But stealth didn't matter, if anybody was waiting for him they would be wasting their time a mile away from here . . .

Until the gamekeeper suddenly found himself face-to-face with a bearded man wearing a Tyrolean hat. The other's features were flushed and not solely from his attempts to negotiate this dense woodland.

A hand was held out, there was no mistaking its significance. Meekly, Reuben surrendered the dead goshawk. He did not protest, even when his gun was demanded. Perhaps for the first time in his life the gamekeeper had run out of plausible explanations.

Swift left the courtroom immediately after the hearing, did not stop to confer with Timpson. It would not have resolved anything.

Reuben had been found guilty of killing a protected species, that was the only consolation. The judge had been lenient, a city man out of touch with conservation who probably didn't realize the seriousness of the offence. A £400 fine and he had not revoked the gamekeeper's firearms and shotgun certificate because Reuben had pleaded that guns were necessary tools of his trade. There had been a disturbing look of relief on Reuben's face that boded ill for the future. He might not even be sacked by the syndicate which employed him. He had been given a licence to kill, it had not been taken away from him.

In much the same way, the ranger reflected, that the goshawks had been reintroduced to their ancestors' habitat to kill.

The balance of Nature teetered on a tightrope. Would humans and those species whose survival depended upon predation, be able to maintain that balance which was vital if the extinction of any creature was to be avoided?

Man had destroyed the rabbits with the introduction of disease over four decades ago, he was responsible for a decline in the fox population by integrating urban foxes into the countryside and thereby weakening the hunting genes of the species. The goshawks had decimated the songbird population in these hills. The hawks would multiply, their need for natural food would be even greater. Were they necessary to the rural scene? Swift didn't know. Nobody did.

Only time would tell.

Garn and Ka hunted Manquhill and Cornharrow unmolested that Winter. The snows came and then melted in the warm, moist winds of early Spring. A pair of long-billed curlews arrived from the coast in search of an inland nesting site. Their presence was noted by Garn and Ka but curlews are masters of camouflage. A search by the hawks failed to find them.

Ka built her nest near to the top of the tallest fir and laid her eggs. Garn would have need to hunt with grim determination once more. There were still a number of rabbits around the scree and grouse in the heather. He was no conservationist; humans had given him his freedom to kill.

Nature's cycle had begun again.